Odd Magics

Tales For The Lost

Sarah A. Hoyt

Goldport Press

Contents

The Rain Of Frog

H enrietta Ford was not the sort of woman who had hallucinations. In fact, hallucinations—which she didn't have! —were some of the many things that seemed to make life far more interesting for other women. For instance, take her mother. Her mother had dreams. Prophetic dreams. She'd come to Henrietta in the morning, from the time Henrietta — Rietta to her friends — had turned fourteen and say "Henry," — which of course was what mother called her — "I dreamed you had married a prince."

At which point Rietta, who didn't follow that kind of magazine, reviewed in her mind all of the dwindling number of eligible royalty in the world, none of which were anywhere near her age, looked her mirror and sighed. There was nothing wrong with Rietta's looks, mind you. At fourteen, she'd been skinny, with a mop of red hair, and a sprinkle of freckles across her nose. The knees of her pants were usually ripped out from climbing trees, her elbows were scuffed from the same endeavor, and her conversation was of trees and hiking and books. Perhaps a very outdoorsy prince, she'd told herself.

But despite her filling in a bit and acquiring curves, and the freckles fading when she stopped spending quite so much time outside, no royalty — or principality — materialized outside her door, on one knee, diamond ring extended. Even if mom still expected it daily.

Her friends growing up, all also had *things*. Her friend Mary, for instance, had been very fond of music. So fond of music, in fact that she pursued it up hill and down dale, despite the fact that she had no musical talent whatsoever. Rietta had often wondered if music should take out a restraining order.

Of course, the obsession had paid off as one of Mary's music masters had fallen in love with her and married her. And it must be true love because he thought Mary played beautifully.

Jenny... Jenny was into history. She volunteered at the museum, collected artifacts, and talked of people dead 100 years as if they were friends down the road. She'd met a nice gentleman while walking a civil war battlefield, and they were now married and had three little girls.

Nelly in her turn had loved money. And she'd married a very wealthy man.

The point being they'd all married and moved away. That morning, on waking up, Rietta was conscious of a great feeling of loneliness.

She'd moved out of mom and dad's house — as she should have — at twenty-five, and had her own little house, on the edge of town. She did very well from drawing/painting whimsical fairy tale scenes, which she sold at local markets and science fiction gatherings.

You'd think that since her "thing" was old fashioned fairy tales, the really interesting ones, she'd have met an ethnologist, or an anthropologist, or perhaps a fantasy fan. But somehow, it had never happened. And it wasn't like Rietta was that ugly. At thirty-four, she was spare but "handsome." Which meant she wasn't pretty-pretty, but also not ugly.

On her way to the shower, she passed by her little sunny studio, and glared at the work in progress. It showed a messy young woman, her flowery skirts flying in all directions, as she bent down to kiss a frog who wore a crown, and who looked very surprised at the imminent osculation. It had struck Rietta as funny: the expressions, the movement, the exaggeratedly bright fabrics. But now she wasn't so sure. She wondered if maybe she should take a day off. Of course, as a freelancer she didn't get paid for work she didn't do, but all the same...

She was coming out of the shower, towel around her hair when the phone rang. Grabbing it from the bedside table, she heard mom's alarmed voice, "Henry, you must not go out today!"

"What?"

"I dreamed there was a rain of frogs!"

"Mother—"

"Henry, I tell you, I'm absolutely sure. There will be a rain of frogs. And think how disagreeable it would be."

Since a rain of frogs was only slightly less likely than Rietta marrying a prince, Rietta smiled and nodded. Then realizing her mother couldn't see her, she said, "All right mom."

But she didn't promise. And besides, she could take a day off without going out.

Which brings us back to the fact that Henrietta Ford did not hallucinate. She also didn't daydream. Outside her little paintings, she didn't even have much imagination.

But there she was, standing in her kitchen, having a cup of tea when a very large — VERY LARGE — frog dropped down, just past her window. He landed on his toes, settled his considerable bulk — he must have weighed almost two hundred pounds — turned baleful eyes to her and said "Croak" in a distinctly tired voice.

Then he pulled on a string, which unrolled a rope ladder from somewhere above, climbed up it laboriously and, ten minutes later, dropped down, landed in front of her window, looked at her and said "Croak."

Again, he pulled the string—

On the third repetition Rietta had had enough. This couldn't possibly be happening. There weren't frogs that large. This had to be a frog suit — a very convincing frog suit — and she wondered if her mother had told someone about the rain of frogs, and he'd decided— No!

She put her cup down on her tiny kitchen counter, and walked briskly out the front door, careful not to stand where the frog would drop, if indeed he was dropping. He did drop, close enough that she felt the wind of his passage. He turned towards the window, looked startled, then looked at Rietta as she cleared her throat and said a very loud, "Oh."

"Look, what is this?" Rietta asked. "Is this a joke? Why are you wearing a frog suit and jumping in front of my window."

He looked confused, then embarrassed. Then he sighed, which was a very weird thing for a frog to do. "I— Look, there was a rain of frogs ordered, but I was the only one available, so they sent me, figuring it was by weight, see, and I counted for hundreds of frogs."

"Who sent you? Who ordered a rain of frogs?"

He made a gesture somewhere skyward.

"Why the frog costume?"

"It's not a costume. It was the taxes," he said. He sighed again and looked very tired. "Look, we'll just assume I'm done with the rain, okay. I'll go back—" he waved at the ladder. "And figure out what they want me to do next. It's probably something stupid. It's very weird being caught in a supernatural incident in a world that doesn't believe in magic. It's tiring too. I could kill for a cup of coffee."

"Uh," Rietta said, and because this was quiet the weirdest thing that ever happened to her, she lost her mind and said, "You can come in and have a cup of coffee, if you want."

Probably the thing that made her believe his story for the first time, was the fact that he wiped his feet... er.... paws... er flippers on the entrance rug.

He made polite conversation too, about how pretty, and picturesque Rietta's little Victorian cottage was, and how nice her kitchen was. She didn't take him to the study. The last thing she needed was for him to see the painting and get ideas.

While he had coffee and she started on her second pot of tea — just to make sure she wasn't dreaming — he explained what had happened to him. "It was her taxes. I mean she told me she was a witch, but I thought she meant Wiccan. I mean, she had crystals and stuff all over her. People do. You don't take them seriously. You don't think they are supernatural, you know? Nobody does."

She watched fascinated, while he held the cup of coffee in both flippers and managed to drink without spilling, despite a marked lack of human lips. "Oh" he said. "You have no idea how much I've missed coffee."

"Where do you live?" She asked, fascinated. It made no sense, but it none of this made sense. "I mean, when you're not raining."

"I don't," he said. "Not in any sense of the word. It's like .... being asleep or better not existing. So, what happened was this, I did the woman's taxes, and it was okay, but then she got audited, and she came to my office. And she said I'd be a frog. And then next thing I knew, I was being awakened for the purpose of showing up in some mountain and croaking to scare a silly hiker into running into the arms of her true love. Then there was this time I had to steal someone's ball..." He waved his hand. He really looked very tired. "And then I woke up knowing I had to rain in front of your window."

She took a sip of tea. She thought of telling mother this and knew she couldn't. "You're not.... You're not a prince, by any chance?"

He laughed, which frogs shouldn't be able to do. "No. I'm an accountant. Though my name is Prince. I mean, I'm Oscar Prince, nice to meet you." He extended a flipper.

"Henrietta Ford," she said. "Rietta to my friends." And she shook his flipper. It was surprisingly non-slimy.

He tried to smile, but frogs don't smile very well, and he looked bashful. "Well, I guess I'll go. Thank you for the coffee, Ms. Ford. I'll go see what damn fool thing I wake up for next."

"Wait," she said. She'd never done anything crazy. She'd never taken any chances. She cleared her throat. "You don't think you'd come back to human if.... if someone kissed you?"

He opened his mouth, closed it with a gulp sound, then shook his head. "More likely if I did someone's taxes," he said.

"But you.... don't know?"

He sighed. "Not as such, but look, lady, I was no prize even when I was human. And now I'm a giant frog. Which woman would be crazy enough to—"

And then Rietta was. She thought it couldn't be that unpleasant. It was a couple of seconds. So, she leaned forward and planted her lips on the frog's forehead — fortunately the giant frog was short, being a frog — for a couple of seconds.

He said "Oh" and gulped. His skin felt very warm. And she opened her eyes to find there was a naked man squatting on the floor of her kitchen, and she had just kissed his forehead.

As for being no prize, he was tall and tanned, and had a mop of curly dark hair — she presumed it couldn't be cut while being an amphibian. Since frogs don't in fact have hair — and blushed very deeply as he figured what had happened. But his eyes were a nice chocolate brown. He covered the essential with his hands as he looked at her and said, "Wow.... I.... I don't know what— You wouldn't have a blanket or something?"

He'd worn her robe, until she could buy him pants, and because this wasn't a fairy tale, they didn't get married.

He'd gone back to the big city from which he'd disappeared, and calmed friends, relatives, and employers with some story.

Only within six months, he'd moved to Rietta's little down. Just down the street from her in fact. "With telecommuting an accountant can work practically anywhere," he said.

He'd formed a habit of coming by for breakfast. Rietta found she was comfortable telling him everything and anything, and he loved her paintings, and talked to her about his more difficult clients. They had a similar sense of humor.

About a year after the rain of frog, they got married, much to the gratification of Rietta's mother who said, "I always knew you'd marry a prince." Rietta had smiled and nodded.

In the fullness of time, they had three little boys who liked hiking and climbing trees and who were forewarned magic was real, and they should never, under any circumstances, do tax preparation for witches.

The Glass Shoe

The house looked familiar and reassuring. It was six years since Aimee
had last been here, and yet it looked exactly the same as when she
used to stop by to see grandma right after grandad died. When she was
fourteen. And then less often though high school.

It was a blue Victorian, set back from the street. There was a tall birch
in the front yard, and a bench on the front porch. Reaching back to
memories, before grandad got sick, she remembered her grandparents
sitting on that bench on Sundays, reading.

She remembered it so hard that she could almost see it: both of them
sitting there, smiling at her as she approached.

When she was very little grandma's house had meant cookies, and
malted milk, and being indulged in a way her parents would never do.

Now—

Now she was afraid of what was inside that door. She'd called grandma,
once a month or so, the last six years. But it wasn't the same. And now
Mrs. Jones, who looked after grandma said that she was losing touch with
the real world. That she might be gone any minute.

The truth was that Aimee had problems with death and ending.
Not just death and ending of people but of everything. Cats, dogs,
relationships.

She'd thought the world was safe and predictable until ten years ago,
when mom and dad divorced. Then there had been her high school
friends, until the group dispersed as if it had never been. Then—

Then college friends for a little while. And then work.

Until the last year. In the last year, it seemed to her half of her friends had got married and half had left for parts unknown. The last year had been hard, between moves and breakups, and— Well, Brad!

And on that moment, as she sat, parked in front of the house, her cell phone rang. She watched, without answering, as Brad's name came up on the screen, and that goofy picture of him that she'd taken a year ago, at breakfast at the diner.

After a while the phone stopped ringing, and there was a ping, announcing he'd left a message.

Right. She was going to go in and see grandma. Mostly because it would be easier than listening to that message.

She slipped the phone into her pants' pocket, picked up her purse, and got out of the car.

Mrs. Jones was around fifty years old, and a widow. She lived down the street. Mom had told Aimee about her, and how she was perfect to watch grandma, because she had training as a nurse. And then the other lady, whatever her name was, stayed with grandma at night.

Mom had arranged it all by phone, from California.

Aimee couldn't really throw stones since she also hadn't been back to see grandma in much too long.

Mrs. Jones greeted her with a smile, anyway. "You must be the granddaughter, Aimee."

Aimee smiled, as Mrs. Jones stepped back into the cool hallway with the marble table by the entrance, where the mail used to be set down. It was now clean, gleaming.

Mrs. Jones led her across the living room.

"Does she know I'm coming?" Aimee asked.

"Well.... Yes, we told her. But she's talking about the ball again."

Aimee blinked. "The ball?"

Mrs. Jones looked over her shoulder, a diffident smile on her faded countenance. She reached up, to pull strands of salt-and-pepper hair back from her face. "Yes. I mean, you know," and then, obviously realizing that Aimee didn't know, added, "She is in her right mind, you know, but—"

"Yes?"

"But lately, this last week or so, she's been talking about the ball, and she's been trying to find her shoe."

Aimee stared. "She lost a shoe?"

"Well, some things have been given to goodwill, yes, but—" She sighed. "I don't know. I gather she went to some ball with your grandfather? Sometime ago?"

Aimee didn't know. She remembered her grandfather as a kind gentleman who smelled of pipe tobacco and always had a sweet about his person for her. That and crispy five-dollar bills, which he doled out like he had a printing press in the basement.

Which she was almost sure he didn't. It occurred to her, as she went up the dark stairs, with family pictures – mom and dad's wedding, her baby picture, the picture of her brother who had died ten years ago, just before the divorce – that she really didn't know that much about her grandmother. Despite all the times spent in this house, eating cookies, reading comic books, talking about what fascinated her at the time, she really didn't know much about her grandparents. They'd always been old, in her mind. Though she supposed they'd only been in their late fifties when she was born. And that was not old. Not really.

Grandma's room was bright. The windows were open, and the late spring air blew through. If there was a smell underlying it all, it wasn't the smell of sickness so much as the smell of chemicals. Grandma's old dressing table, by the door, the one she remembered playing at when she was still a toddler, had been divested of all its sweet-smelling powders and floral perfumes that used to fascinate Aimee, and instead was crowded with medicine bottles.

And grandma was by the open closet, rummaging.

She didn't look like she was dying, despite what grandma had said on the phone. She looked older, of course. Like time had taken all the spare softness from her, dried her out, leaving only essence of grandma. Like she'd been dried and toughened and reduced to her absolute central core. But she was standing on her on her own feet and looking through the closet.

She turned and smiled, "Aimee." She came close and hugged Aimee, in a fluid movement, and that close she smelled like the perfumes, of roses with a hint of lavender.

"Grandma."

"Let me look at you." Smile. "You're all grown up. You remind me of your mom when we met her."

"Mrs. Jones says you're looking for your shoes? Something about a ball?"

Grandma looked as if she'd been caught out in something she hadn't meant to be discovered. "Let's have some tea," she said.

And Aimee remembered that's what they'd done, last time she'd been here, just before she left for college. They'd had tea and the special, "for good" bought cookies that came in the tin. That's how grandma referred to them, and she always thought they were better than the ones she made.

This time, the tea was the same, and very sweet. Grandma got the good teapot out, and the saucers cups and plate from the matched set. "This was my wedding set," she said. "I've put it down in the will for you."

"Grandma, I don't—"

"Oh, I think I've used it maybe a dozen times in my life, most of the time with you. It doesn't matter. You should have it."

Grandma poured two cups, but she seemed to just wet her lips with her tea, and not really drink it. She didn't eat any of the cookies. Aimee didn't know how to ask about that. Mom had said, "She's stopped eating. Since you're in Denver for the new job, you should go see her. It might be the last time."

Aimee offered the cookie box, feeling stupid. Mrs. Jones had made herself scarce.

Grandma smiled, "No, thank you, honey. I'm not hungry. Tell me about you. What are you doing? Your mom said you had a job?"

"Uh.... Yeah. It's just an entry job, you know, executive assistant, and... well, that's what it is."

"And there's a young man, your mom told me."

"Well, there was..."

"But?"

"But he wants to get married."

"And you don't?"

"Well, not yet. Not at twenty-four," she said. "I mean, it seems like we should.... Do things, learn who we are first."

Grandma wet her lips with the tea. "You're running down the staircase," she said.

Aimee had no idea what Grandma was talking about. And it got worse from there. Mrs. Jones ducked in and said something. Her sister had called, she had to go. Could Aimee stay a few hours? She gave Aimee her phone number in case of emergency.

While they were talking, grandma made it back up the stairs. It seemed to Aimee if she were dying, she wouldn't be able to walk all over the house.

But Mrs. Jones looked worried about leaving her alone, and Aimee smiled and said, "Never mind, we'll be all right."

Then she went up the stairs, after grandma.

Grandma was at the closet again. "The problem," she said turning to Aimee. "Is that I can't find the shoe. And I don't think they'll let me in without the shoe."

All right. Aimee had no idea what that was all about, but then – she glanced at the dressing table – all those tablets must have weird side effects. Aimee remembered how she had hallucinated all sorts of odd stuff when she'd taken pain killers.

"All right. How about you sit down on the bed, and tell me what you're looking for, and I'll look? What do these shoes look like?"

Grandma's closet was scarily large and very full. One shelf was taken entirely with sweaters, which she remembered grandma wearing all the time, except in the height of summer. But there were things hanging that had to be older than her: A beaded skirt, a beautiful, embroidered dress. The shoes were under everything on the floor, she knelt down and started shuffling through them, then stopped when grandma said.

"Not shoes. Just one. He has the other one. And it's glass."

"Like Cinderella's?"

"Exactly like that." She paused a while. "You see, I went to the ball and met your grandfather."

"You met him at a ball? Or was it prom or something?"

"No, no, listen, not this world. The real world. It was a ball. He was the prince, and he sent a notice for every young lady to come, so I put on my glass slippers, and I went."

"What? No fairy godmother?" Aimee asked, feeling discomfited. She'd read somewhere that when people had dementia you should just humor them. But Grandma didn't have dementia, or at least no one had said she did. Still. What was the use of arguing.

She looked over her shoulder and grandma looked pensive. "No," she said. "I think they added that in afterwards. I just had to find my glass slippers, and I stepped through and…. It was beautiful, Aimee. Really beautiful. There was this castle, which was made of glass, only it was white glass and…. Well, it sparkled, all of it sparkled.

"And everyone wore these wonderful gowns, but he came walking through, and he chose me. We danced all night." She paused. "Only I knew that I couldn't stay in the real world. Sure, no one dies in the real world. But no one lives either. There are no babies born. There is no time… So, I chose time. And when I chose, the clock struck. And I ran. I lost a shoe. And the other one, I kept. It's in the closet. It should be in the closet."

Aimee, knowing it was crazy dug through the closet. There were leather pumps, and crocodile-skin shoes, and a pair of red patent leather stilettos she couldn't even imagine grandma wearing.

"He came after me," grandma said. "That's how you know he loves you. He comes after you to this world."

Aimee looked over her shoulder again, and grandma was looking straight ahead. She sighed. "It was a good life, Aimee. Even if your brother left us much too early, and then your mom and dad couldn't deal with it."

"And then dad died this summer."

"Yes, but that's the risk you take when you leave the real world. And it's still worth it." She sighed. "Only now he's waiting for me, you know? He's gone back to the real world, and he's waiting for me. At the passage. He has the other shoe, but I have to take the one I have. It's the only way to go over."

At that moment, Aimee's hand touched the thing. She knew it before she pulled it out from the corner, where all the skirts hung to the floor and hid it. She felt the glass, cool and very smooth, and pulled it out, and there it was. A pump. Size seven, like the other shoes. But all made of glass. Only it couldn't be glass, could it? It had to be crystal.

"You found it."

Aimee was very careful with it, handing it over. Grandma took it. She was speechless for a moment, then she said, "I knew you'd find it. Probably just like your own pair." She turned it over and over in her hand, then looked up. "I think I'll rest a little bit, before getting ready for the ball."

When Aimee left the room, Grandma was half-sitting half laying against her pillows, holding the glass shoe.

Aimee went to the kitchen, and washed the tea things, then listened to Brad's message. "Aimee, please call. If you want me to move there, I'll move there. I don't need to date other people. I know what I want. I want you."

That's how you know it's real, Grandma had said. They come after you.

She felt suddenly very sleepy and lay down on grandma's sofa, like she used to do when she was little.

She was putting glass slippers on. She was sitting up and putting glass slippers on. And grandma was standing there. She was barefoot, but holding her slipper. And she had on the beautiful, embroidered dress. It hung kind of loose on her frame, but it still looked beautiful, all white and gold.

Grandma smiled at Aimee. "I thought you could wear my wedding dress," she said. "I've saved it all this time, and I thought maybe you could wear it. You can't go to the ball in jeans." But she didn't have any wedding dress. She just stood there, waiting, as if the two of them were late for something.

So, Aimee got up and followed her, and grandma was moving like she was much younger, towards the little room at the back, past the kitchen, the one with the books and the sewing machine.

Now there was a great light there, and the sound of voices, and music.

Aimee saw grandma step through what looked less like a doorway, and more like a big tear in the wall. Someone she only saw as a shadow was there, and he handed grandma something. It must be the other shoe, because grandma stopped and lifted her feet to put shoes on, and then she gave the man – yes, it was a man and he looked like pictures of grandad when he was young, tall, and straight and dark haired – her hand, and the two of them stepped through into the crowd. They both looked young and beautiful. They turned to each other, and—

"Grandma," Aimee stepped after, walking into...

It was a glass castle, only the glass was also light. And her own glass slippers tinkled on the floor as she walked. Looking down, she saw that she was wearing a white lace dress. She could feel something like a tiara in her hair.

"Aimee!" It was Brad's voice, and she turned to him. It was Brad, but also it wasn't Brad. It was Brad as he would be if he were perfect, wearing a tux of a deep sparkling blue, with a crown on his blond hair, which for a change lay perfectly straight, instead of half up in the air, as always.

She forgot grandma, and grandad, and she danced with Brad.

She didn't know how long they danced, but everything was perfect. And she, who could never run without falling was dancing the waltz as if she'd been doing it her whole life. Around her were beautiful, happy couples. She thought she saw her brother. Only John had died when he was single, but here he was dancing with a beautiful young woman, a stranger. Then she caught a glimpse of grandma and grandad, enthralled, in each other's arms.

And the dance was more than a dance. It was being together, really together, as you couldn't be ever in life. It was.... The real world. Where everything was magical and perfect.

Someone stood up from a throne she hadn't seen before, and a voice rang out. It was male, and in her mind, she knew it was the voice of the king. He said something about all the couples here, all perfect, all forever.

"But ...but no one lives either. There are no babies born. There is no time... So, I chose time." Grandma's voice sounded in her mind. And Aimee realized she could stay here. Here forever, in perfect harmony with Brad. But she'd never live. Yes, sure, she'd never lose him. She'd never lose a child as she'd lost her brother. And they'd never divorce like mom and dad had done.

But they'd never live.

"So, I chose time."

Time. There must be time. A place ruled by time, where love was far more perilous, but also... grew. And there were children, and laughter, and a good life. It was worth it.

She heard, somewhere, a clock strike, and everyone stopped in their dance.

Time. She had to choose time. She had to leave the real world.

She pulled away from Brad – it was the hardest thing she'd ever done – and she ran.

She ran across the beautiful ballroom and down what seemed like an endless staircase made of glass. She lost a shoe halfway down, and saw ahead of her, the rent in the real world that led to grandma's sewing room. She plunged through it and felt the second shoe come off her foot as she ran through.

And there were sirens.

After the ambulance had taken what remained of grandma, Mrs. Jones made tea, "There's no reason for you to blame yourself," she said. "She went in her sleep. And you slept too, and that makes sense, seeing as how you drove all the way from Denver. But there's nothing you could have done. She stopped eating three days ago, and she didn't drink either. It was just her time. She missed your grandad."

Aimee nodded, dumbly. "Did you... They didn't take the glass shoe, right?"

"A glass.... Shoe?"

And Aimee thought she'd probably dreamed that too, just like she'd dreamed the ball and grandma and grandad twirling together.

While Mrs. Jones was washing up, Aimee went up the stairs. She couldn't imagine the paramedics taking the glass shoe in the ambulance. But it wasn't anywhere in the room. She looked everywhere, even under the bed.

She must have dreamed it. It was all a dream.

Her cell phone rang, and she picked it up, and turned it on without thinking. It was Brad, "There you are," he said. "I'm coming up. You'd best give me your address, or I'll go door to door with these glass shoes till I find you. And there's a lot of doors in Denver. It could take forever."

"Glass shoes?"

"You lost them, in the staircase."

"But that was a dream," she said.

"Maybe," he said. "But I was also in the dream. And I have a pair of glass shoes. Your grandmother told me to tell you she's okay. And that I am to come to you and stay with you. Because it's worth it. I wouldn't dream of disappointing her."

"You can't have had the same dream I had!"

"No? then how do I know what happened."

"Oh," she said. And she gave him her address.

There was time enough for the real world. She'd keep the glass slippers. But meanwhile they'd live and love, and have a few babies, maybe.

And some day she'd find the glass slippers again and step through to the ball that never ended.

Eggs

I t was Halloween night and there was a horse at my door. Or at least a horse's head. And he was carrying a basket of candy. And he stood six feet tall, wore a wine-colored sweater, artistically ripped jeans, and expensive tennis shoes.

I sighed and started to close the door, and the horse said, "No, Eileen, listen." He lifted the basket, "I brought candy for Tori and Talon."

I sighed again. I hadn't seen Paul in six months. The lawyers had almost made everything neat and ready for signing. Seeing him at the door hurt. I didn't want it to hurt. On the other hand, really, he had never been abusive or done anything that justified keeping him away from the twins. Particularly on Halloween.

On yet the other hand, they'd been asking where dad was. Particularly since they couldn't trick or treat, not really. Not like they were used to in the suburbs. It's not that there was no trick or treat in rural areas, but as cold as it was, and with snow falling, I wasn't about to drive them the half a mile to the next neighbor and then the mile to the neighbor after that and so on. Besides the fact that the rural road was not paved, and there was a significant fall off on either side.

"How did you get my address?" I asked. Not that I'd ever expected Paul to stalk me, but for various reasons, including being a woman living alone with two small children, I'd never publicized my address and the farm was bought under a corporate name, of which I was main holder, with shares devolving to Tori and Talon if something happened to me.

He hesitated. Don't tell me how I could see. There was this expelled little puff of breath, and he shuffled his weight from foot to foot just a little, then he huffed, reached up and pulled off the horse's head, to reveal an embarrassed face. Also, ridiculous. His reddish hair was all on end. And he'd lost weight. And not in a good way. He opened his mouth, closed it. "My mom gave it to me."

I almost asked him if he was wearing the wrong part of his horse's costume. His mom had died three months ago. But Paul had been very close to his mom, and he wouldn't say that as a joke.

I made a face. "Okay, but you come in, you give them the candy, you talk a little and you leave, understood? And then it's every other weekend, and I'll bring them to you, okay?"

He nodded. It was less a nod and more just moving his head down fast, then up again. "You moved to the middle of nowhere," he said.

"Kind of had to. To do something I could do from home that would feed the kids. Besides the school here is great." I closed the door behind him, and he put the horse's head on the hat tree in the entrance.

It reminded me of other times. Like when he'd come into our suburban condo, at this time of year, and removed hat and coat, and the kids would rush to him.

"But there's no trick or treat," he said.

"Oh, we had trunk and treat at the school parking lot earlier," I said.

We'd come to the end of the hallway, and he hesitated. "To the right," I said. "They're in the kitchen, coloring while I make dinner."

He did that almost-nod again, and walked to the right, where the stub of hallway opened up into a vast eat in kitchen with a big wood stove. It was warm and well-lit and the kids were working so hard at their coloring books they didn't even look up.

Until Falada came charging in, of course. They say geese are sometimes used as guard dogs. I believe it. She came charging at Paul's legs, head down and honking, like she thought he meant to take her eggs. Which she probably did think.

"Whoa," I said, stepping out in front of Paul. "Whoa, Falada, easy, it's a friend."

She stopped, confused, because I was her safe person, and therefore I wouldn't be protecting a bad person. Her head turned up, her beady eyes focused on us, and she made a weird honking sound that was probably a swear word in goose. Then she waddled back to the basket, by the dinner table.

Paul's voice sounded a little squeaky as he said, "You have a goose in—"

And then the twins were on him. I remember it like a slow-motion sequence. First Talon saw him and jumped up, "Dad!" and then Tori. And then they were all over him, clambering up. He dropped the basket, and took them, one in each arm, saying things like "Whoa," in the same tone I'd used for Falada.

The kids were telling him about the trunk or treat, in a big jumble. And about the school. And how this house had coops in the back where we kept the geese, and why Falada was in the kitchen.

"'cause she's having her babies out of season, 'cause she's crazy, and mom said—"

He walked to the table with the twins one in each arm, and somehow managed to peel them off and onto their chairs, and admired the "Halloween princess" coloring book my mom had sent Tori. Think a little girl in various gowns, surrounded by pumpkins and bats and black cats. Talon, bigger and more introverted than his sister waited silently to show his dad his own Halloween Avenger book. Yeah, super-hero like character, pumpkins, and bats and such. Talon colored it in tiny minute strokes always within the lines, and was starting to work on shading. Tori, on the other hand just colored really big, never mind the lines and as long as there was plenty of pink and sparkly crayons, she was fine.

She was also pushy and obnoxiously loud, and — as her mom — I say that with love, interrupting Talon's explanation of why he'd used a darker color in the background with a shout of "Look, dad, she's got sparkles on her cloak" and shoving her little face forward, with a big gap-toothed smile.

Paul said, "I brought you candy." Almost as an afterthought, retrieving the little basket and pushing it into the middle of the table. Even from where I was, I could see it was about half Pixie sticks which were Tori's most favorite thing ever.

The kids looked at it, and then away, and continued chattering at Paul. He had this big stupid smile on his face.

I couldn't tell him to leave. I was going to have to invite him to dinner. The kids really had missed him. I didn't want to think about that. The papers were almost ready. And it's not like I'd just decided to leave him, okay? He had been dating the nanny. While married to me. But the kids were his, and—

I took one of those deep breaths that seem to never end, and turned back to cook. After a while the kids settled down a little, and Tori went to get their favorite book — the big, illustrated fairytale book Paul had bought them for Christmas last year — and asked Paul to read. I didn't actually remember his ever reading to the kids.

Okay, sure, he might have. It's just that with the kids being small and both of us having had demanding jobs, we'd tried to take turns staying home with them when the other was working overtime. We had a nanny for the daytime, and then after work, one or the other of us stayed home. It occurred to me, suddenly, that this was a stupid way to run a marriage. But—

The twins were pressed on each side of him, while he read. He was doing voices. I took the big tray of meatballs out of the oven. I'd planned on two meals from it, but of course, with a man at the table.... So, I did two packages of spaghetti and started making the marinara.

Timing worked out right. Paul had just finished The Goose Girl, when I said, "Tori, silverware, Talon plates."

"Four, mommy?" Talon asked.

"Of course." I tried to remember when the last time had been we'd eaten together. I'd moved out six months ago, and before that—

Talon was reaching for the step stool when Paul picked him up and reached him to the upper cupboard for the plates. Talon grinned his own gap-toothed smile, "Thanks, dad." Had he got quieter these last six months? He'd never been garrulous, mind you, but—

Dinner was loud and boisterous as I didn't remember it ever being, and Paul was funny, and kept making voices, including giving Falada a voice, when the goose made soft sounds, in her sleep on the eggs.

"How many eggs is she hatching?" he asked. "And couldn't you have used an incubator?"

"Sure," I said. "But incubators are ... Well, you have to turn the eggs at the right time, and it's more work for a single person, who is busy with other stuff, you know? This way Falada does it. It's just inconvenient for her to become broody in October, and just before the big snow storm."

"I thought all geese did this on a schedule," he said.

I shrugged. "Some critters are mixed up, you know? Anyway, I was about ready to consign her to the thanksgiving oven, when lo and behold, I found she'd been hiding eggs and had a clutch and was sitting on them. All the other geese hatched in Spring, they're full grown, so I brought her indoors. She's a pretty good guard dog."

He looked worried. "You guys are living so isolated..."

He didn't say it seemed strange to him, considering how close to Denver we used to live. Tori asked him about bats — no, I don't know why, my daughter was like that — and eventually Talon told him a long and complicated story about the bat cave, at the end of our property.

After a while, food was eaten and the kids were starting to nod off, with sauce all over their faces. To my surprise, it was Paul who said, "Go wash up, and into jammies, okay? I'll come and tuck you in when you're ready."

I started putting away the leftovers, and he started to pile the dishes by the sink.

"So, about your mom giving you my address?"

"I was going through her things," he said. "You know, my sister already went through, but she asked me to go to the folk's place and see if there was anything I wanted to keep. So, I took the day off yesterday and went to do that..."

"And?"

"I fell asleep on the sofa. There really wasn't much, by the way, though I found some books... Anyway, I fell asleep on the sofa, and I dreamed she was giving me a royal talking to." He paused. "I guess because I had talked to the lawyer earlier, and he said it would be ready to sign on Monday. You know. So, I fell asleep, and she said I should talk to you. She said I'd been miserable, and I should talk to you or... Or I'd never forgive myself. And the kids might never forgive us. And I said I didn't know how to talk to you, I didn't even know your phone number. So she said look at the calendar. So I went and looked. And she'd written your address down."

I hadn't ever given my mother in law my address. But lying wasn't one of Paul's abilities. No, seriously. That was part of the reason I'd left. I'd asked him if he loved Iris, and he'd just got all red and tongue tied. Remembering that put pepper in my voice as I said, "And what does Iris think of that?"

He looked startled. "I have no idea. I haven't seen her since you moved out." He paused. "Well, since the month you and the kids moved out. Took about a month. We went for coffee, a couple of times, and I took her to dinner, but..."

"But?"

"We had nothing to talk about. And she wanted to do things."

"Things?"

"Go to a concert. Go to a movie. Stuff like that. I just.... I didn't care that much."

"But you were in love with her."

21

He chewed the inside of his face. I knew that expression. He used to do that in college, when he was trying to figure something out. "I thought I was. Turns out it was just she was the adult companionship around, outside of work."

I had been all ready to wall myself off, to be all remote to say, "You only came here because she left you." But I had realized earlier we'd been raising the kids in the most stupid way possible. And we'd thought ourselves so smart, too. You know, we could both have high powered careers and still raise the twins. Brilliant.

"Do you miss work?" he asked.

I shrugged. "Weirdly no. Surprising amount of work in a goose farm. I do miss adults sometimes. Did you— Do you often read to the kids?"

"Sure. You?"

"Yeah, but—"

"But the other was never around to see it," he said. "I realized that about a month after you left. I missed you, you know? Mom was right. I had to tell you. I'm sorry. I was an idiot. I mistook someone always there and willing to listen for love. Mostly we talked about the kids. And we never did anything, you know. Stuff. I just took her out for coffee sometimes, when I got out of the office, and you were at home. I shouldn't have." He gave a half laugh. "The weird thing is I mostly talked to her about the kids."

"You could have talked about that to me."

"I know." He pointed at the goose. "I'm like Falada, you know. Doing things all out of order. Just a crazy critter, I guess."

He got me to smile, before I could stop. But then I said, "If we stop the process, it's going to take a while to restart."

"Or — we don't restart?"

"But— I invested everything I could spare from my dad's inheritance on the farm. I don't want to close it." I paused. "Besides, I don't want to go back to living the way we were."

"No," he said. "I.... I got permission to work from home. If you.... If you don't want me to move in, I will find some place to rent around here."

"There's nowhere to rent around here. Everything is twenty miles away." I paused. "You probably shouldn't drive back, anyway. It's snowing hard out there, and that road isn't safe. You.... could stay in the guest room tonight, and we'll talk it over in the morning."

He nodded and got up. "Let's load the dishwasher. Tomato sauce sticks like nobody's business."

I started rinsing while he loaded, and as I handed him the last plate, he said, "I do love you, you know. I always did. I really never fell in love with Iris. I just thought I had. I was just so lonely."

I sighed. "I still love you," I said. It came off very curt. "I almost didn't let you in because of that." I paused. "And that probably is more than just today. I was afraid, you know. If I gave you too much, if I didn't have a fall back. I could end up like mom, when you left me for the younger chick. And then Iris." I felt tears in my eyes, and he must have sensed it, because he put his hand on my shoulder. "Hey," he said.

"Right," I said. And with the last of my strength, "Tomorrow. We'll talk tomorrow. The guest room is near the kids' rooms. Did you bring a change of clothing?"

"Just the horse's head," he said, making me snort.

Which is why the next morning, I found him, with a sheet wrapped around him toga-style making pancakes for the kids while his clothes tumbled in the dryer.

Turns out it's much easier to look after the kids when you both take turns, at the same time. And even easier when you actually talk to each other.

Which is good because there were three more kids in time.

By the time Falada the goose died of old age, Talon and Tori had finished college and the others were in high school.

We stuffed the horse's head and mounted it over the fireplace. It didn't tell us that either of our mothers' hearts was breaking, but every time I looked at it, I thought of my mother in law with gratitude.

I eventually saw her calendar, and there was indeed my address, under "Aileen" written on the calendar in her handwriting, the way she wrote things she didn't want to forget.

It was in July. On the day she'd died. But she'd been in the hospital for a week, after a stroke. I had no explanation for it, but I was grateful anyway.

In some other time line, we got divorced. And maybe we fell in love later with other people, who knows? But what was the point of finding another love, when the love we had was perfectly fine?

I kept the calendar page too. Framed. Over my desk. Some people believe around Halloween the world of the dead comes close to that of the living. But no one ever said anything about ink and paper.

And it doesn't matter. Marriage, like an egg is a mystery. You treat it right, you trust it, and in the fullness of time something wonderful bursts forth.

Even if sometimes someone needs to nudge it at the right time.

Mirror

S o, maybe it was just a dream. I know that it can't be real, right?
I think it started because everything was going wrong in life.

Lately the mirror had become an enemy. I looked into it and didn't recognize the reflection: it was a person with faded hair, and loose skin. There were wrinkles on her forehead, and her eyes had lost the shine that had got me those contracts selling mascara.

I'd stopped putting makeup on, not only because it seemed to look funny — like a painted skull — but because I couldn't stand looking at myself in the mirror.

Peter laughed at me. "Relax!" he said. "You look fine," he said. "You're fifty and you look thirty. Stop behaving as if you're a decaying crone."

Mind you, he was older too, but men get more handsome as they age. They become distinguished and gain authority. Women on the other hand, as I told him "Are like summer roses, and as a chill sets in we just look faded and brown and ugly."

"What?" he asked. "You're taking up poetry, now?" And he kissed me, and when he kissed me it was all worth it.

"Perhaps the obsession with being old is because Liddy is away at college?" he asked. "Go visit her for the day."

And I had. And that only made it worse.

You see, Liddy was my vindication. Liddy was my proof I'd been right all along.

Mother had been very upset, when I decided to quit modeling and get married at twenty. She said I was just at the beginning, just starting to make it out of local markets. That spread in Teen Chic was only the beginning of success. I was going to go all the way to the top and make millions for one sitting. And then maybe work in movies.

But I'd met Peter. And I loved him. We were going to get married and have a dozen children.

The dozen children never came. Only Liddy. But Liddy was.... perfect. Oh, not as beautiful as I'd been. Or at least not as beautiful in a less conventional way. Instead of my oval face, my blue eyes, the hair that had once been a bright gold, she had Peter's round face, and very white skin. She had dark air, and dark eyes, and a mobile mouth always disposed to smile.

Mom sighed when she visited. "Pity she took after Peter," she said. And, "Unfortunately her face will never be her fortune."

So, instead of being dragged to beauty pageants as soon as she was out of diapers, my daughter had learned to read at four, and she'd learned to play piano — all by herself, with just some video for help — at six, and she sang like an angel, and she was brilliant, truly brilliant. She liked building things, and she wanted to study engineering.

At the end of high school MIT had accepted her, and Georgia Tech had offered a scholarship.

She'd chosen the state college, instead, just an hour away, because her high school boyfriend, Mike, was going there. I'd bit my tongue really hard, but I figured she could always go somewhere better for graduate school.

And she seemed to be enjoying school. And making friends. Only it left me very lonely, I guess. Peter told me to just find something I liked to do, and asked if I wanted to go back into modeling, since I was still a very handsome woman.

But I looked in the mirror and frowned, and I knew I was no longer "the fairest of them all."

So I drove out to spend the day with Liddy. We went to the zoo, where we used to take her when she was little and then we went for a walk in the park. And that's when she told me.

When Peter came home, I was sitting in front of the mirror, tracing the indentations on my forehead that would become furrows soon.

He didn't talk. He sat on the bed. And I told him.

"Liddy is pregnant," I said. "She and Mike want to get married this month. And then she'll drop out. He's going to finish his degree, but she—" My aged face looked even worse while crying. "She says she can get some work in the evening, playing piano in restaurants and stuff, while he stays home with the baby, and then...." I was fully crying now. "She says she just wants to stay home, and raise her kids."

Peter looked troubled, but didn't say anything. He folded me in his arms, until I'd stopped crying, and then we went to bed.

It's a thing, even after thirty years of marriage, that no matter how bad the day has been, when I hug Peter at night, under the covers, it's like we're in a paradise of our own. We drift to sleep as if we existed in a place with no time, as if this, just the two of us, warm, together were the best eternity.

Only that night I couldn't drift off to sleep. So I put on my sweater, and my jeans, my boots and my heavy coat. I put my coat and gloves on.

Outside, it was snow and blowing wind, and it was near midnight. But our suburb is very safe. Just a dozen houses, in the middle of wooded land. And perhaps if I walked enough I could sleep after.

I walked out, into the sting of wind-driven snow, and I walked and walked. I felt as empty and barren as the landscape outside. I'd had so many dreams for Liddy. I'd given up so much for Liddy. And now instead of being my vindication, my proof I'd been right all along, she was just going to be a suburban wife and mom, like every other wife and mom.

What had the point of my entire life been? I wish I could go back, take it all back, start anew. And my heart was prey to a darkness darker than the night, to a fury greater than the wind that blew grains of ice into my face.

I'd just said that, in a low and vicious voice, "I wish I could take it all back and start again," when I heard the wheels behind me.

You know those fairy tale illustrations, where the carriage looks like a pumpkin, only it's all gold, and the tendrils that would be stem and leaves are golden ornament?

There was a carriage like that, coming up behind me, in our perfectly mundane suburban street. It was pulled by four horses so white that they seemed to give off light, and so perfect they didn't seem to be flesh and blood.

The carriage slowed down — the dark caped man driving it said something I couldn't understand — and then it stopped, and the door opened.

I stepped back, because pumpkin carriage or not, I, like every child of the twentieth century, knew not to get in a vehicle with strangers. Only the person inside was no stranger. She made that clear, as she leaned forward and said, "Isabelle, get in here right away."

And it was mom. Only it was mom as I remembered her, when I was very small and she was young and always put together, make up and hair and clothes always perfect. Not the mom who'd visited in the early marriage, not the mom I remembered, really. But mom.

As I scrambled into the seat, I realized other things. She was wearing this amazing dress, all blue and silver, as though it had been woven of moonlight, and she wore a tiara made of the brightest silver, and covered in pearls.

The smell, in the carriage, too, was as I remembered when I was very young: the scent a mix of mom's perfume and face powder. It was a fragrance of roses at their peak, all woven with dream. When I was little I'd thought that was the smell of adulthood and of being beautiful, and always put together perfectly.

Inside the carriage, it was very comfortable, like riding on a cloud and I wanted to ask mom how she'd got this pumpkin carriage, and where had the horses and coachman come from.

But instead she said, "So, are you done with your little adventure?"

I blinked at her. "Adventure?"

"This whole, *I want to live in the mortal world*, thing, daughter. The, *I don't mind if I die, I'll live forever in my children*?" She laughed, and the laughter too was as I remembered from childhood, the tinkle of crystal, the sparkle of ice. "Are you ready to come home?"

"Home?" I said.

"Oh, of course, the spell. You don't remember." She leaned forward and touched my forehead.

And then I remembered. Only it was weird, because I remembered my "real" life too, being a child model, and the pageants, and all that stuff. Only at the same time I remembered. Really remembered.

I'd been a princess of fairyland, daughter of immortal Titania, worshiped and loved by the whole court. I'd danced away every night, laughed away every morning. In the vast, dream-like landscape of fairyland, I'd seen my reflection in lakes and ponds, and it was always perfect of course.

I didn't know how long I lived, or how many centuries, because every day was unchanging and perfect, every morning dew-washed, every night blue velvet with the diamond pin prick of stars, and no problem was bigger than what to wear for the ball that evening.

And then Peter had come. Strong and raw boned, with a round and ruddy face, sparkling black eyes, hair that wouldn't lie down right, and a mouth disposed to smile.

"That ridiculous boy would fight every dragon to get to our inner keep," Mother said. "And I'd still would have sent him away empty handed. Only you wanted to live in the mortal world. You said your children would live after you, and that this too was immortality."

And I remembered. The argument had shaken the crystal columns and made the white ceilings tremble. And I'd left with Peter. On his steed. Well, okay, actually his mustang convertible. Or at least that's what it was outside fairyland.

We'd kept that car going too, for near thirty years, and Liddy still had it, though it was much the worse for the wear.

"So," Mother said, leaning forward. "Are you ready to come home?"

I leaned back on the seat. Mother looked at me avidly. She was not used to not getting her way. In this my real world memories and the spell both agreed.

And something tugged at me, something misgave in my heart, like when you're about to jump, and you realize it's too long a jump and you'll fall. Not that this ever happened in fairyland, where every jump was perfectly timed.

"I can't go back," I said. "I'm not the same. I'm so old—"

"Not in fairyland," she said. "You will be as you always were." From beside her on the seat, she pulled a mirror, and she handed it to me. And there I was. No wrinkles. No loose skin. Just my face as I remembered it, my face as I always knew I was, somewhere, inside the aging body.

And it had all been a mistake, hadn't it? Liddy was not going to be my vindication. She might be smart, and she was beautiful to me, and she'd been given so many gifts, but she was going to throw them all away and live a small life, in a small way. It had all been for nothing and I was aging, and would die. And I didn't even know if there was an ever after for the likes of me.

"Do humans live after death, Mother?" I asked, suddenly.

She shrugged. "They think they do. It's not for us to know."

"Do we?"

She laughed. "We do not die."

And there it was. We do not die. So supposing I died as a human, would there be anything after? Even the humans didn't know.

It had been yesterday, it seemed like, in my mind's eye, that Peter and I had ridden away, on his steed. And I was already old. And what had I done with my life? I'd raised a daughter, who was going to do nothing with her life, but raise children and—

Mother knocked on the ceiling, and the carriage slowed. "I have to give them time," she said. "To open the silver gates of fairyland."

We'd go in. Past the guardian dragons. And the gates would close. And I'd dance away the nights, sing away the mornings—

Peter would wake and know himself abandoned. And what would Liddy's son or daughter look like? And would she have more?

She and Mike weren't going to have a lot of time. Perhaps we could take the kids, now and then, and go to the zoo, as we had with Liddy, when she was small.

And there would be a bit of fairyland in their laughter, the tinkle of merry bells, the sparkle of silver and they would laugh and dance, and then grow up and—

The carriage had slowed. "Stop, stop I must get out."

But Mother knocked on the ceiling. The carriage picked up speed.

And I opened the door, and jumped out.

I hit the ground hard. Probably would have broken something except for the snow. I rolled, and got up, feeling hurt and cold.

Why had I jumped? Why? What sense did it even make? Why trade perfect eternity for a few good moments, and then regret and failure?

I managed to pull myself up. My hip hurt, and my side felt bruised. But the carriage was nowhere in sight. Instead, I was at the end of the subdivision, a mile and a half from home. An easy walk which I often took in summer.

Across the street from me, the lights of the convenience store sparkled. I didn't have a cell phone, and thought of going in, and asking them to call Peter to come and get me. But that was stupid. He'd be asleep. He didn't deserve to be awakened.

And the walk back would give me time to think. I limped back, through the snow, and thought, and thought. You know, eternity of perfect everything was.... eternity. And I'd always be young there. But there was an intensity to the moments of happiness and triumph in the human world. And I had eternity whenever Peter held me.

But no. A temporary eternity made no sense.

I was about halfway home, and saw someone coming towards me, through the white blizzard. He was big and bulky. But our suburb was safe, so probably someone like me, walking to calm down.

Then he drew closer, and I recognized, Peter."

He said "Belle" at the same time, but instead of rushing to me, he stood.

I went to him, gave him my hand. He took it. I felt his warmth through the snow. "I woke, and I was all alone," he said. "And I thought you'd left, you'd gone back home to your mom."

I raised an eyebrow at him. "My mom?"

"To fairyland."

I felt a little shock. It must have shown. He smiled, "Of course I remember. It was only you who had to forget so you could leave." He paused. "I saw a drawing of you, when I was twelve. In an illustration of fairyland. And then I had to go in. I had to win you. My own piece of immortality."

I walked forward, then, and he held my hand. "I'm sorry about Liddy," he said. "I knew you had great hopes for her."

"I still have great hopes for her," I said.

"Now, Belle," he started. I remembered vaguely, in my earlier rage of crying, talking of abortion of adoption, of—

"No, not that," I said, quickly. "I think that was the fairy. As a fairy, you don't have much will of your own, you know. So you expect your children will be like you. You plot their courses and they'll be exactly as you expect." I paused. "And even then, you can be wrong. Some young man might come in and fight the guard dragons...."

He laughed and I said, "Yes, but you know, that's part of it. I don't get to choose her path. It's not fairyland where every day is the same. This is what she chooses, the dragons she must slay."

"But you had hopes—"

"Sure, and maybe she'll do something absolutely wonderful, some day. Or maybe not. Maybe in time between childhood and death, she'll just be happy. Maybe that's all it is. Even if you don't do much, really, but take the kids to the zoo, and read to them, and listen to them laugh, and feel happy."

He looked at me worried, then, "Have you been happy?"

I laughed and kissed him. "Maybe we should sell the house and move closer to Liddy. Remember how tired we got when she was little? We can have the kids over now and then. We can take them to the zoo. We can read to them and play with them."

"Yes", Peter said, and smiled. "We can love them."

Later, when we were in bed, after the passion had been spent and I was warm again, as he was half asleep, I snuggled up to his warm, familiar form, I thought that, yes, maybe that was all it was.

Maybe there was no other life after decay and death for me. Maybe there wasn't even one for humans. But here, together and warm, here was happiness. Here was the certainty of love that outlasted decay and death. Here was eternity.

I needed no other.

Rumpled

S he was crying in the copier room when I came in, and she looked up at me with moist blue eyes, like pansies under the rain.

I couldn't remember her name. Too D*mn Young was what I had tagged her as, but that isn't a name. Even my name is not that weird. Crying like that, she looked about sixteen. No makeup. Blond hair down to the middle of her back. Very pretty. Maybe one of our high school interns?

And then she grabbed a tissue from box on the shelf, wiped her eyes, blinked at me and said, "Oh, Mr. Rumple, I'm so sorry. I didn't know— It's just I don't know what to do. This promotion."

And I realized she couldn't be

an intern — they didn't get promoted — and that she knew my name, which probably meant she'd been kicking around the office for more than a year, because I didn't come in that often. I'm just the accountant, okay? Mostly I work from home, or come in after hours to look through the books. Sometimes, rarely, I have to come during the day for some documents. But not that often.

Now she was more composed, I upgraded her age to early twenties.

"You're crying because you had a promotion?" I asked.

She nodded. "It's Maddie," she said. "She says I was being oppressed by remaining a receptionist. She said that receptionists are outmoded, and I need to work as— As a copywriter."

Maddie, which is what all the young women in the office called her, was Ms. Madeline Maddoc, AKA Mad Maddie to all the male members of the staff. Mad Maddie had struck again.

Look, I'm not sure what had happened to poor Mad Maddie back in the dim years of her youth, before she'd become CEO of Baileng Copyrighters Inc. Maybe a man had bit her, or not bit her. Whichever.

What I know is that if allowed to go on at any length in a staff meeting she'd bore you with a long list of men who had made discouraging statements about her abilities, starting, seemingly, in her cradle. At one of the meetings I attended, I swear she said that the doctor who delivered her said, "Well, she's a girl, she'll never amount to much."

At any rate, the mad one had achieved control of the company by age 40. And since then she'd been on a mission to make sure none of the women hired by Baileng ever had to suffer in an inferior position. If this meant promoting the cleaning woman ahead of our top copywriter? Well, so be it. Girl power!

Look, I didn't care. I was the accountant, and no one in the glitzy daylight business cared much about what I did in the dark after hours, with our books, provided it wasn't criminal and the IRS didn't take enough taxes to shut us down.

The problem was that what Maddie had done was make our company near-unable to keep decent female employees, from receptionists to executive assistants to — even — cleaning ladies. If you weren't hiring for top posts, you might as well hire a man, or else you'd not have the employee long. She'd be promoted up the ladder, fail, and leave, either in disgrace or for a better position, aka, to be someone else's problem.

But no one dared explain this to Maddie. She'd tell us again about how her science teacher had told her girls were stupid at math, which frankly sounded pretty unlikely for the 70s in the US.

"Ah...." I said, noncommittally, and prepared to back out of the room, except the young woman was actually very pretty and seemed devastated. "And you don't think you can do it?"

The tissue came out and pressed against her nose. "I don't know anything about advertising," she said, nasally. "I have an associates in English, for crying out loud."

"Well.... that means you know how to write in English, so that's a beginning. You'd be amazed how many of our executives can't do that. Between the impacted and the incentivized, they verbify the language to death."

This got me a pallid smile, around the tissue. "She brought me in to the meeting, and she made a big song and dance about the Straw Brothers account and how I was perfect for it. I had no clue what to say, so then I went to my desk and looked it up. It's a lumberyard in Caroline. She wants me to do a big advertising campaign for their straw bales. Apparently they have a big straw bale event every fall, and they hired us to— to—"

"Promote it?" I asked, helpfully. To be fair, this was pretty small potatoes, which meant Mad Maddy was moderating her reach somewhat. Maybe old dogs did learn new tricks. This thing was probably worth maybe ten thousand for us.

She threw her arms wide, "Why would I know anything about straw? I was raised in Denver."

I shrugged. "It's just Maddie. Look, it's not as scary as it seems. Yeah, Straw Brothers has stores all over the front range, but I doubt they'll pay us more than about ten thousand for a campaign. I'm not even sure why they did it. Maybe they're looking for a deduction. People do buy straw around this time of year, for animal fodder, and to cover fields, and to do straw bale gardening, because it's apparently better if it rots a bit over winter, and stuff. But it's a pretty closed market that's going to happen anyway. I don't think you can fail."

She made a face, "The only time I saw a straw bale was when we went to this cowboy pancake breakfast, when I was little, and we sat on bales." She sighed. "I still have no idea what to do. They want to do some kind of TV spot?" She started crying again. "I don't know what to do!"

I normally don't get involved in this stuff. The faster Mad Maddie's pushes fail, the less damage they do. But the kid was young and looked scared.

"Okay," I thought of a way this couldn't be claimed to be sexual harassment. Us ugly guys can be accused just by staring vacantly in a woman's direction. And as ugly guys went, I was the ugliest. "Look, if you want to spitball, we could maybe grab a coffee. Or not. Entirely up to you."

"Would you? Let me throw ideas at you, that is?"

"Oh. Sure. I'm just here to pick up some stuff, and it will only take me about ten minutes."

"Okay!" she said, and grinned, and looked like I'd promised her something wonderful.

So she grabbed her laptop, and we went to the coffee shop across the street. Her name was Amber Golden, and she was 25. I didn't even ask her any of that. And I also didn't do much in the way of suggestions, honest. It's just she was really creative. I was just there to listen, and the fact that I couldn't help being delighted with some of her ideas made it better.

You see, the kid was good at doggerel rhyme and line-cartoons. She kept drawing these funny figures doing funny things, and explaining what they were doing with silly verses. In the end she concluded by pointing out that straw bales were great for seating and tables at Fall and Thanksgiving parties, and really, who was I to argue.

I took her funny rhymes on Straw for Pa, and asked her if she wanted a tune for it. Look, something you accumulate over a few thousand years of life is music. At least if you have a memory for it. Her rhyme fitted perfectly to this jingle that medieval maidens used to dance to.

I hummed it, then she got up some sort of program that I could play it in, and which would record the tune. And then I showed her a program that took line drawings and animated them, and was free, even.

By the time she had a great spot, about two minutes long, there was a server standing by our table, all serious, "Sorry, guys, but we close at seven, so—"

So, we'd taken up a table and only bought two coffees and a couple of pastries. I gave him a generous tip, to compensate, while Amber gathered up her stuff, and thanked me all confused, "Thank you so much, Mr. Rumple. Is that what I should call you, Mr. Rumple? And gosh, I don't know how to thank you."

I laughed. "Oh, just give me your first born," I said. "And call me Rumple. Just about everyone does. Also, I didn't do much for you. You did it all yourself. All you needed was some self confidence."

She grinned and skipped away, and I shook my head. There were echoes and memories in my mind, but it had never gone well for me, so why would it now? I wasn't even going to try.

Over the next month our paths didn't cross, although I heard comments from some people about the new Golden kid. But perhaps it was the "new golden kid" and might not be amber at all.

Then about a month later, when I was leaving the office, I heard her call, "Mr. Rumple?"

I turned. She was wearing nicer clothes. Still a skirt suit, just nicer. I was just glad she hadn't gone to pantsuits. Those weren't designed for the female anatomy and always looked weird.

She blushed. "I... I have a new marketing campaign they gave me? Achyro restaurants.... and.... well.... I wonder if I could take you to lunch and talk to you? It seemed to help so much last time?"

We went out to one of the Achyro restaurants, Achyro Diner, and stuffed ourselves on dolmades and baklava, while she told me her ideas.

Not line drawings, that time. She was thinking of taking various members of a large family, and showing them celebrating their occasions with Achyro restaurants, from the young couple with kids going to the diner for their pancake special, to the young man proposing in Achyro Heart which was sort of a bistro-ey thing, to— You get the point. Ended up we stayed through lunch, and then with the complete campaign sketched out, she invited me to for dinner to celebrate.

Of course I was wary. I really am very ugly. Or would be, if I were human.

Somehow, and I swear I made no moves — and kept expecting some sort of trap, honest — this became a thing. Every week, she'd take me out somewhere — she was very insistent on paying — and talked to me about her projects.

"It's just, see, that I feel very comfortable with you," she said, after a few months. "I don't have any family, you know? Mom and dad died in an accident when I was young, and grandma died three years ago. With you, I feel like I'm with family."

Which figured. I wanted to tell her I wasn't family. I wasn't even really human. I was... Lonely. Really lonely. I looked back over the last few thousand years. There used to be more of my kind around. Now, it was just me. It had been just me since the few remaining of my kind had died in the black plague, leaving me all alone. That's when I'd tried that foolish gambit. I kept wondering if she'd connect the dots.

And I thought she hadn't. We went out all the time for six months. Then she invited me as her plus one to the company's Holiday dinner. People kept looking funny at us, because there she was, five eight and blond and beautiful, while I was five four and.... well, very ugly indeed.

Then she asked me out to dinner, and came in looking all serious, and told me some guy named Walter Furst had asked her to marry him. I felt my heart sink to my feet, and she looked at me, all serious, and said "You know.... the thing is.... I mean..... Would you be all right with that?"

"Only if you give me your first born," I said, and grinned, displaying teeth that I knew were just a little too sharp for humans. Most humans backed away from that, but instead, she reached across and grabbed my hand.

I was so shocked, I didn't even pull away. She looked straight into my eyes and said, "It wouldn't work. I know your name. I mean, your real name."

And then she said it.

I want to assure you that the legend about my vanishing in a puff of smoke was embroidery on what actually happened. Though I might very well have thrown a massive snit, because I'd worked so long and so hard and then—

This time I just blinked at her. She smiled at me, "Yeah. I looked in company records, after our first meeting," she said.

"And?"

"And it doesn't matter to me. I was just hoping you wouldn't want me to marry Furst. I was hoping—" She took a deep breath, "But I didn't know what the whole thing with the first born was...."

"Oh," I said. "Well, most of my kind — there is no name for us, really. Though elves or fairies or whatever fits, if you don't go thinking of us as Tolkien elves — died in the Bubonic plague. Maybe all of us. I don't know. I've never met another. I just... I was lonely. I thought if I raised a baby, I'd have a family. Okay, it was stupid."

She gripped my hand harder. "We're not so different, you and I. I mean, I'm not an elf or anything, but you always felt like family."

And I realized suddenly that's what she'd become. Family. Kind of an important part of the family. We'd encouraged each other, supported each other, joked together. The last few months what had been my very lonely life with numbers for company had been... well, kind of the life I wanted. I sighed, "You'd marry me?"

"In a minute!" she said.

That's when I lost my mind and kissed her. Afterwards, as I laughingly told her that we couldn't get married in a minute, but I thought we could in 24 hours, in this state, she looked serious again, "You won't dye your hair white or something to pretend to get old along with me, right?"

I grinned. "Oh, no. Solved. You see, if we marry a mortal, we become mortal."

She pulled back. "I couldn't let you do that. Trade immortality for me?"

I laughed. "A worthy trade. Better a few years with you than endless, lonely immortality."

That was when she kissed me.

I did get her first born, it turns out. And the second and third and fourth. All of which look like their mother, fortunately.

And she knows my name, of course. My name is her name too.

Mrs. Rumplestilskin has never complained.

Blizzard

I'm not actually stupid, you know, and I did grow up in Colorado. As far back as I can remember we used to joke that weathermen in the area go stark raving mad, and that we could get a better weather forecast by flipping a coin or using another form of divination than by listening to the so called experts.

When I was seven there was a snow storm on my birthday. Which wouldn't be all that weird, except that my birthday is on the fourth of July. Oh, and the storm was in the morning and by evening it was 80 degrees.

When I learned to drive at 16, mom always made sure even if I was just driving the two miles to the grocery store I had space blankets, water and power bars in the car. Summer and winter. Just in case, you know?

And in winter? In winter you were never safe. You could start out from home in clear blue skies, as I had this morning, only to find yourself, 2 hours later, stuck in a car with your asshole brother, with the snow coming out so fast that you were crawling bumper to bumper the length of Colfax avenue, unable to see the car ahead of you at all, and just sort of hoping those fuzzy lights shining through the whiteness were far enough ahead that you couldn't accidentally bump it. Oh, and hoping that a red light wouldn't come on somewhere and force you to stop, because you could feel you were skating on a layer of fast-forming ice over the snow.

And your brother was lecturing you on critical theory or some equally insane bull and telling you that you simply didn't have the mental capacity to understand his objections to visiting dad before the surgery.

At which point I might or might not have said that I didn't know what possessed me to come into Denver to try to convince him, when he'd hung up on mom a dozen times, and I knew he was an asshole.

But I knew exactly why I'd come. Mom had got the Irish up.

Don't even ask me how she can get the Irish up, okay? So far as I know, her mother and grandmother were born in the US. Mom said there was Irish somewhere in her family tree, and it was kind of hard not to believe, what with that peach-perfect pale skin, the blue eyes and — when she was young — the pitch black, straight shining hair.

But I swear to you that when she got the Irish up, she got a lilt of an accent, and her eyes shone a certain way, and she would say things that made absolutely no sense except in some "ripped from a fairytale told in the green hills of Ireland for century upon century, and probably going back to some bard who had a bit too much of the mead."

The words fae and fated would come out of her mouth, then. And it was absolutely terrifying. Not least because of how often she was absolutely right, even if it made no sense.

So, as I sat at the kitchen table, in the farmhouse, and she brought the pot of coffee to the table and set it on the coaster, and pushed the sugar bowl towards me because she knew I liked my coffee sweet enough for the spoon to stand up in, and she told me about how she couldn't get Nort to answer the phone, and she couldn't tell him about dad's surgery. I'd been stirring the coffee harder and harder, till all the particles of sugar were a distant memory, and refraining from saying the word that started with *a and rhymed with pole* because it upset mom, when mom's voice got that weird Irish lilt, coming through the genes or something, and she said, "It's not his fault poor boy. He's got a shard of ice in his eye."

At which point I stared at her a long time, then snorted, even though I knew it wasn't safe to snort at mom's notions, not when she had the Irish up. "Mom, if you mean that Doctor Norton Blizzard is a prisoner of the snow queen, you kind of need to rethink it. I don't think he's had a girlfriend since... High school?"

Mom looked at me with that vague pitying look, her eyes still as blue as the blue in our enamel cookware, and like all of a sudden she was sorry for me too, and said, "But that's just it, Lexi. That woman.... his advisor when he went to college, what was her name....? Can't remember, but she got a shard of ice in his eye. Since then he sees everything through that shard of ice, and he can't get free. The world is an endless frozen place, all bound up in bloodless theories that never applied to any real person ever. And he can't get free. Or love anyone. Even himself."

And she was serious and tragic enough, I was just grateful she'd spoken in modern words and not broken into any kind of rhyme or song.

She was serious enough I'd gone into town to see Norton and have a talk with him. In November. On a clear, brisk cold day in November. Which frankly was just asking for trouble.

And now I was paying for it, stuck in a car with my brother, taking him from the university to his apartment. And it wasn't even going to be any good, was it? because he was spouting nonsense about how dad was privileged and therefore would get the best healthcare possible, and the nuclear family was a trick of the patriarchy.

And I was cutting between the road and glancing sideways at him, wondering where my brother had gone, and what had happened to what used to be a very fine mind.

You see, my brother used to be my hero. I suppose it's inevitable, when you are ten years younger than your big brother, despite all attempts by your parents to have kids in between the two of you. You might be spoiled and cherished, but you're also going to revere the one who was spoiled and cherished, and your parents' only child for ten years before you were born.

And Nort, you know, he was okay. Oh, right, fine, he was great. He was the type of big brother who never got tired of playing with his bratty little sister, let the sister follow him everywhere, and got looked at funny by his friends because of the little creature at his heels.

And he was smart. Really smart. He was helping in the farm by the time I was born, of course. Farm kids learn to drive the tractor as soon as they can look over the windshield. And anyway, he was big for his age. And dad trusted him with stuff, and discussed stuff with him by the time he was 12. That wasn't surprising. But he was book smart too. And he somehow found time to read .... well, everything. And remember it. One of my early memories was his getting books in the mail from the interlibrary loan program, because he'd exhausted our little library. And then mom and dad got him a computer, so he could take some classes on the net, remote, because he'd run past all the stuff in our school. And it wasn't all Greek and Latin and poetry — though he liked those — but math and physics and all that.

Even though I was much younger and a girl, I'd never been the favorite. Mom and dad looked at Nort as if they were in awe of him. Like they weren't sure why they'd been given this really special son.

The best part is I didn't even mind. I was in awe of him too. I took him to show and tell when I was in kindergarten, and just had him answer questions, to show how smart my brother was. And he let me, which meant he was kind too. And not just to me. He always noticed if someone was sad or feeling down, and found the right way to cheer them up or look after them, without seeming to be doing it. Like when he'd noticed mom was not feeling well before thanksgiving and convinced her he really wanted to learn to make the apple pies mom always made, and then made her sit down and give him instruction, so she wasn't on her feet.

And then he'd gone to college. And mom said he'd got a shard of ice in his eye.

The last time he'd been by — not for thanksgiving, because it was a colonialist holiday — he'd lectured dad — who already wasn't feeling too great, though we didn't know why — on how dad was a white oppressor. And when dad asked who he was supposed to be oppressing, out in the middle of nowhere Colorado, and paying the going wages when he needed help, Nort had raved and ranted about institutional privilege. And when Dad said that no, it was just hard work, and look at North, he'd worked hard and now he was a professor in Denver and had a much better life than our parents, Nort had said that all those books mom and dad had arranged for him to borrow, and the computer, all of it was white privilege, and that Dad was a white supremacist.

Which is when dad had said something, I don't know what, because I couldn't hear it, that had made Nort storm out of the house.

And now he was telling me why he wouldn't come and see his own father before the surgery that might or might not remove most of dad's stomach cancer.

"Until Father educates himself and understands his white privilege, he—"

Which was when I — having checked that we hadn't gotten any closer to the snow-fuzzy lights in front of us — saw the glint in his eye, just at the edge. And heck, it looked like a little shard of glass, or ice. It was so close to the edge of the eye, so close.

I checked in front of us once more, still stuck in a long line of cars, still unable to see much of anything, still praying a car going through a cross street wouldn't T-bone us.

And then I heard mom's voice. He's got a shard of ice in his eye.

I did what came naturally. In between his "So, if father only apologized" and his "For his privilege" I leaned over, reached, and slapped the back of his head with all the force that had made me a menace at softball.

I turned back ahead almost immediately, but I was aware he stopped, there was a pause. He didn't even say "ow" and was just blinking eyes, really fast.

Looking down, I saw something glittering on the console between us, picked it up, and put it in my pocket. The weird thing? it was about the size of the very top of my pinkie, but cold radiated from it, making my whole thigh numb.

"Why did you do that?" Nort asked, sounding vaguely surprised and hurt, but not angry at all.

I considered about ten different answers, then I said "Mom said there was a shard of ice in your eye."

This time his voice was also not angry, but vaguely puzzled, "I wasn't captured by the snow queen."

I didn't say anything, because it would sound demented. And besides, the little shard of ice was almost painfully cold through my jeans. What would it be like to have that in your eye?

Also, the snow was slowing down, clearing, and I could see a little ahead, which was a relief, and we were almost at his place, in a high rise near City Park. He'd only got in the car with me because the snow was starting and there was no uber in sight.

He didn't say anything a while, either, and then said, "I don't have a car, you know? It's not worth it in good weather."

"I know," I said.

He cleared his throat. "Is it really serious? Dad, I mean?"

"Yeah. they think it hasn't metastasized yet, but there's some shadows, so they won't know for sure until they cut."

"Damn it, I thought.... I don't know what I thought. It's all... cold and fuzzy. Like I wanted to be really all pure reason, and no emotion. I don't know." I slid into a parking space in front of his building, the operative word being slid, but we didn't hit anything, because the whole street was more or less deserted.

"If I get an overnight bag, will you... I mean, I'll need a lift back tomorrow, or to rent a car or something."

"No problem," I said. I'll bring you back.

"I won't be a minute."

*****And he wasn't a minute, and dad was really happy to see him, and no privilege or skin color were mentioned at all. In fact, Nort came to the hospital when dad went in for surgery, and spent a lot of time there, until dad was sent home again.

It turned out they got all the cancer too, so dad had chemo, but it's now been three years with him cancer free.

Nort changed a lot after that, became more like the brother I remembered. He quit academia, too, and decided to put his physics degree to some sort of use in industry, not that I get it. I think part of the attraction was working from home, because he got married a year after that drive in the sudden blizzard. They're coming for thanksgiving and bringing their week old infant. Mom and dad can't wait. Okay. I can't either. I always wanted a niece.

And okay, you can say maybe it was all because he was so shocked I smacked him, that it knocked some sort of sense into him.

But I never told anyone, not even mom, about that ice shard. You see, it was still solid in my pocket, in the hot car by the time we got to the farm. And yeah, I thought of just throwing it out, but we have a lot of wind, and what if it blew into someone else's eye.

So while Nort was visiting with Dad, I'd put it in a pan, on the stove. It took a long time to melt, but when it did, I poured it down the sink, straight into the sceptic tank.

Where no one else can get that particular shard of ice in his eye.

And I never told mom, because the last thing we need is for her to get her Irish back up again. It's bad enough she's been telling me about Paul, the guy who came to fix the tractor last week, and dropped by yesterday to make sure it was still fine, and how she has a feeling—

Just because he stayed for dinner, and asked if I might maybe want to join his gaming group.

Mom makes no sense sometimes. But she's scary when she gets the Irish up.

Awake

She was going down a magic path, and then at the end there was a spindle, and she'd pricked her thumb. She remembered dad reading about it, when she was very small and sat on his lap.

No. She'd never touched a spindle in her life. She'd been in the car, driving with mom to take things to her college dorm—

No. She was in the museum, and she was 10 years old, and they were talking about how people used to make thread and showing how to use a spindle.

No. She was on a magic path going through a magical forest, all green and gold, and at the end there was a great light, and there she lay on a glass coffin. She walked, in fascination around her own coffin. She was wearing a white dress and clutching a white rose.

Suddenly there was a feeling of.... was she being kissed? And then warm water fell on her face.

Helen woke up. For a moment she didn't remember how to open her eyes. There was a smell of antiseptic, and several faint distant beeps. Not too far off, someone was crying.

She blinked her eyes, opened them, flinched at the light, and found herself in an hospital room. She found herself saying "Spindle" only it didn't come out as a word at all, but as a sort of wheezy groan ending in a croak.

Suddenly the room was full of people, shouting, checking her. Someone, a doctor? Nurse? was moving a finger in front of her eyes and asking her to follow it with her eyes.

Later they asked her name and date of birth, and she had to clear her throat and drink water someone offered her before she could tell him.

There was a rush of things, and they rolled her down the hall and into an MRI machine. In the process, Helen realized her hair was too long. It bothered her. She always wore her hair short, because of swim team, and also because it was easier to get ready in the morning. She'd never been a morning person. Now her hair was brushing her shoulders and that was strange. And she had no explanation.

It bothered her all the way to being wheeled back into her room, and fed some fairly tasteless green jello.

Afterward she was left alone and looked out the window at the familiar background of downtown and mountains. only there were a couple of buildings she didn't remember, and no one had told her what she was in the hospital for. She felt like she'd been sick a long time. Like she couldn't quite muster the right strength on her arms and legs, like... Something was wrong. She'd felt like that before, when she'd had that bad flu at twelve, a year after mom remarried and just before she met Drew. Like the flu had drained all the energy from her body. It had come back. She'd been almost fully back to normal a month later, when she met Drew, though she was still weak and clumsy enough she'd dropped her books in the hallway and he picked them up. And she'd looked up into his face, with its too-big eyes, surrounded in a hallo of rumpled dark hair, and read in it the same struck-with-wonder expression as she must be showing. It was like the most ridiculous meet cute ever. She'd never even thought of boys or dating before, but.... Drew was like a long-lost part of her.

Her mom and step dad — she didn't remember her dad except in dreams, because he'd died before she went to first grade — hadn't liked it. Mostly because... Well, Drew just was the son of a single mother, and his mother was a waitress. And drew wanted to be a musician, which mom said translated to bum. They'd made fun of it, but they'd referred to it as puppy love. As nothing much. They'd joked about it for the next six years.

Just before the accident, she'd been arguing with mom because Drew had asked her to marry him, and mom said going into pre-law Helen was just signing on to be supporting a bum musician forever. He'd be out playing bars and hooking up with girls and Helen would just be paying the bills.

But Helen knew Drew, and she couldn't imagine anything more unlikely. They'd talked. He knew few people made it in music, ever, and he was studying accounting, as a backup. He said he was just trying, but if it didn't work, he'd make sure he wasn't a burden. And he'd never really seemed to have any interest in any other girls, just like she'd never had any interest in any other boys. They just weren't like that.

Besides, she had said yes, and she wasn't going to take it back. She figured they'd manage one way or another. But mom said getting married early would just mean that she wouldn't ever go to law school. Helen would end up as a waitress or something. Mom said she herself could have gone far if she hadn't married dad and then been saddled with Helen when dad died in that stupid war.

She stared at the ceiling and wondered if mom was still mad at her. And why was she in the hospital? She wasn't in a cast or anything, so what had happened that warranted a hospital? Had she dreamed up the accident? Perhaps she'd had a flu or something.

She dozed listening to the background noises of the hospital, because it seemed to her someone magically materialized in the room. He was a young man, wearing scrubs, with a stethoscope around his neck and a bright green plastic clipboard. He grinned at her, "So, how is our miracle lady feeling?"

"Miracle? I'm all right."

"Good, good. Any memory problems?"

She frowned. "I don't know. I remember being in a car with my mom, and I think we crashed, but maybe it was a dream. I don't know? I mean, why am I here?"

"It wasn't a dream," he said, the big smile in place. "You crashed."

"Oh. Well, I don't remember anything since then. I mean, a lot of dreams about spindles and stuff, but not...."

The bright smile stayed in place, but there was a wrinkle on the forehead. "Why.... why do you think you should remember anything else?"

Helen reached up and touched her hair. "My hair was short."

"Oh. Oh. Okay, I get it."

He pulled a chair close to the bed, and said, "Okay, this is going to be a bit of shock, so I want you to take a deep breath and be ready, okay?"

She nodded, somewhat afraid. Had mom died?

"You are right to remember the accident as the last thing that happened to you, though it's not quite. When your mother hit the SUV, her car was totaled, your mom was fine, and you looked fine, but you would not wake up. No exam we made, including MRIs showed anything wrong with you, and you were belted in and never hit anything. We thought it might be a spinal injury at such a level it didn't show. Except you'd not wake up. We waited a week, then a month, then we gave you stimulants, but you did not wake up. Your brain activity was the same it would have been if you were in a deep sleep. You reacted to pain or cold, by moving the part pricked with a pin, or exposed to cold, and sometimes you smiled or frowned, though it seemed to have no relation to external stimulus. And you would not wake up."

"For a month?"

The young man — was he really a doctor. He looked barely older than her 18 years of age — frowned. "No, Hel— Ms. Cockaigne. I'm sorry, we got used to calling you Helen. But.... Ms. Cockaigne, you have been asleep for ten years."

She didn't know what she told him afterwards. She didn't know what happened. She didn't doubt it, though. That explained her hair, the weakness in her limbs. She had a vague idea he'd talked about neuro-electrical stimulation, and why though she'd need physical therapy her muscles hadn't completely wasted away, but she hadn't been fully listening. Her mind had been going through a cycle of its own, spinning over the shock of ten lost years.

Ten years. She wasn't eighteen but twenty eight. And she'd obviously never gone to college, much less law school. She was a high school graduate and twenty eight years old, only her mind was eighteen. In her mind, last week, Drew had taken her to the ice cream shop for her eighteenth birthday, and he'd proposed. She felt at the fourth finger of her left hand but there was nothing there. Well. Hospitals didn't let you keep jewelry, did they? Not that it was anything expensive. Just a little thin twist of silver. He'd told her he'd get her a real engagement ring later. He'd gotten a job doing the books for his uncle's bookstore, and he was saving, so he'd buy her something nice in a month or two.

But her finger felt too naked, and she felt bereft.

It had been ten years. She stared at the ceiling. Did she really expect him to be single, waiting for her? She'd been in a .... what had the doctor called it? persistent vegetative state for ten years.

It hit her suddenly and out of the blue that this must have cost a fortune. Did her step dad's insurance cover it? If not—

Mom had resented Helen as far back as Helen could remember. Or maybe not that, she had resented that Helen's dad had died and left her with Helen. She resented having to get a job as a secretary just to pay for their living expenses. Yes, that was how mom had met her next husband, but not six years, and anyway, mom always said she'd been meant for better things. If she hadn't got married she'd have been a best selling novelist.

Helen tried not to judge, because until she remarried mom had had a very hard life, but all the same, she'd never quite understood what she was supposed to do about it. Other than go to law school and become very rich, and make it up to mom, maybe a bit somehow.

But now—

When a nurse came in with a different color of jello, Helen asked, her voice shaking only a little, "Is.... is my mom going to visit? Did you tell her?"

The nurse looked surprised. "That you woke up? Yes. But you know, she's in Florida...."

So, mom was on a trip. Helen steeled herself for the accounting of how much Helen's stupid illness had cost, when mom got back.

She'd eaten and started dozing, when the phone rang. "Ms. Helen Cockaigne?"

"Yes?"

"I don't suppose you'd give us an interview?"

"What?"

"Well, you know, all our viewers want to know what it's like to be a real life Sleeping Beauty."

"What?"

At that moment a nurse had come in, and talked into the phone about how the patient wasn't well enough for this, and then hung up. Then called reception or whatever a hospital called it and said no calls should be directly forwarded to this room. They routed through the nurse's station.

She'd blushed a little while explaining to Helen, "I'm sorry, but you really do need to rest, and all we need is the phone ringing off the hook, with all the journalists wanting stuff. Let you get a little better first." She was a big motherly woman, and arranged the covers around Helen as if Helen were about six, as Helen drifted off. She supposed, as she did, that of course there would be a human interest angle to someone who had slept for ten years, after all. She imagined she would be some kind of celebrity for a week or so.

Well, maybe she could do fundraisers and take some of the pressure off mom."

And the phone rang. She picked up.

SARAH A. HOYT

"I can't believe you'd pull this, now." It was mom's voice and she
sounded very, very angry. "He put you up to it, didn't he? All for the
publicity and to paint me as a villain!"

"What? Who?"

"Drew Alexander!"

"What? I haven't talked to Drew in.... I guess ten years."

"That's what you say. But my lawyers will hear of this. There's such a
thing as slander, you know?"

The phone went dead, and Helen blinked. What did Drew have to do
with this?

Just then a nurse, this one young and very pretty, looked in and stared
at her. "Ms. Cockaigne— Oh, no." She said, staring at Helen who was still
holding the phone, and she was sure, pale at the onslaught of anger from
Mom. "I'm sorry, she said she was your mother, and I—"

"She was. She is."

"Oh." Then she took a deep breath. "Well, there's someone here to see
you, and he wondered if you'd let him come in. He says if you're very tired
he won't, but he—" The nurse blushed. "Well, I'm sure you'll want to see
him."

"Who is it?"

"Drew— That is Mr. Andrew Alexander."

Helen couldn't find words, but nodded.

Dew was dressed expensively. That was her first thought. He was
wearing jeans and a dark blue t-shirt, but it had that look of clothes that
had actually been fitted and were made of very good materials.

He was.... older. But not old. Though she had to argue with her eighteen
year old mind over that, he didn't look old. He'd just finished growing and
filled in. He was the man the boy had promised to become. But his face
was the same, with the dark eyes too big for him, and looking somewhat
anxious. And his hair, though it was obvious at some point it had been cut
very carefully, was all on end. She smiled, suddenly, finding her familiar
Drew. Drew ran his fingers through his hair while thinking, so his hair
never stayed combed for more than a few minutes.

He stopped at the door, but when she smiled, he rushed in, and pulled
the chair that was on the door side of the bed, not the one the doctor had
used. He removed a book from it, to the bedside, and then sat down. He
blushed a little, under.... well, it was interesting for Drew to have a dark
five-o-clock shadow.

Catching her looking, he gave a chuckle, and ran his hand across his cheek. "I'm sorry, I was on a plane to New York City when they called, and I had arranged to come back. I haven't shaved. It's just good they called before I was on a plane to Germany."

"Germany? Do you live there?"

He laughed. "No.... just a t- trip."

"Oh."

"I can't believe you're awake. I hoped so much, I waited so long." He reached for her hand atop the covers, then hesitated, and she closed the distance, grabbing for his hand. His hand was warm and felt strong, the fingertips calloused.

"I can't believe I've been asleep that long."

"Well, you know how you used to cut corners and sleep only a couple of hours, to study and everything? It just caught up with you." His hand squeezed hers, and she found a little laugh.

"I just feel terrible for giving everyone so much trouble," she said.

He shook his head. "It's not like you did it on purpose."

"My mom called. She thought I had. She said I.... arranged it with you. She said it was slander."

"What is slander? Is she out of her mind? I'm not even giving any interviews."

Helen frowned, "Why would you give interviews? She said her lawyers—"

"Yeah, there's kind of a court case. May I explain?"

"Of course," Helen said. "I'm tired of feeling like I don't understand anything."

"Okay. So...." He took a deep breath. "I'm kind of a pop start."

She blinked. "Kind of?"

"Well, it was like this, for two years after.... well.... you know, after your accident, I worked for my uncle, and I went to college, but I was writing songs and putting them up on you tube, and eventually, it just sort of exploded, and then I got a recording contract, and—" he sighed. "I'll tell you everything, someday, but anyway, I became a pop star."

"That— That's nice."

"It's mostly a lot of work," he said. "And I learned to have agents and press secretaries and lawyers defend my privacy, so I could do the work where it counted: in the songs."

"Yes, of course," she said. So, mom had been wrong. "I remember you always told me that you needed luck, but also a lot of work to make it in music, and that you had to try, but you might never make it, because you didn't know if you could work that hard, even if you got lucky."

He blushed, and squeezed her hand. "I had to. I had someone to look after."

"Of course," she said. She'd been steeling herself for this since she'd found out it had been ten years. But perhaps they could still be friends. She couldn't imagine losing Drew forever. "Of course you're married. What's her name."

He flinched back, "No, of course I'm not married. They don't let you marry people who aren't conscious." And before she could react. "Which was the problem. See, your mom's insurance, or I guess your stepfather's, cared for you till two years ago, when you turned 26, and then your mom said they should let you go."

"Let me go?"

"Stop care. Turn off the machines. After eight years, all the doctors said you'd never wake up—"

"But.... she didn't?"

"No. I...." He blushed. "I asked your mother and step father to let me pay for it. So they let me. But they wanted to move to Florida. They moved to Florida a couple of months ago, actually. And they felt bad about leaving you.... well.... across the country, so they wanted to disconnect you. And I sued to stop them. I've been keeping it tied up in court. Only...." He paused. "Only yesterday a decision came down in their favor. They are your legal guardians. And I had to go on tour. So—" He sighed. "I'm sorry. I came in to read to you, I don't suppose you remember?"

She shook her head. Then she said, "I remember someone kissing me.... And something wet."

He laughed. "Men don't cry, so it couldn't possibly be one of my tears that was wet, but I did kiss you. You know, I thought it was goodbye."

"So, " she said. "That was why you— why the press is calling. You're famous. And the lawsuit."

They were silent a long time. "I know you might never forgive me for all this. I didn't mean the lawsuit to become public. I didn't want to air out everything. I really didn't, but it's very hard, even with all the buffers to keep my life out of the press. I know that's.... You might not want to sign up for that, and I'm sorry I dragged you into it."

He squeezed her hand. "I'll go now," he said. "I think you need to rest."

She wanted to tell him to wait, but her mind was in a whirl. After a while she pressed the nurse's button. "I hear I'm a cause celébre in the press. I want magazines. Do you have magazines and papers about me? About Drew?"

The nurse, the young one, nodded.

She read for hours. Drew had not been public about his attachment to her until her mom had sued to disconnect her from life support. Then it had come out he'd visited her every day of her coma, and read to her. The whole thing had come out, and the press had become very excited about it, because it explained why Drew Alexander didn't have a love life. Because he was in love with this girl who wasn't conscious. The press called her Sleeping Beauty.

And Drew hadn't exactly been very honest with her. The most sensational tabloids pointed out he'd bought her parents a vacation house in Florida for the privilege of also paying the exorbitant bills of her care.

Eventually she fell asleep, but she woke up in the morning, to the excitement of being allowed tea and toast, and felt like she'd been thinking all night.

Drew had invested so much in her, spent so much time dreaming about her. Could she ever live up to it? Or was she just a dream in his head? And did he even still love her, now she'd woken up?

He'd left without saying anything about their relationship.

She had a physical therapy session, and been allowed, or forced to take a few steps, holding on to a walker, which felt ridiculous but was also extremely tiring. She supposed she had to learn to walk again. Stupid the things you forgot.

Back in her room, she reached for and got the book he'd been reading to her. It was a book of fairy tales and the book mark was on sleeping beauty. She read it, frowning. Well, at least she hadn't slept a hundred years. Though she thought Drew had got past enough brambles—

"Knock, knock," Drew's voice from the door.

"Oh," she said, closing the book. "I thought you'd be in Germany."

"No. Cancelled the tour, of course."

"But...." She'd gathered just how big he was from the magazines. "That must be very expensive."

"It's only money." He sat down by the bed.

"Must be nice."

"That part is."

She felt her cheeks grow hot. "I read magazines, and everything you did, and— I'm sorry. I'll try to pay you back. I don't know how but I'll figure it out."

"I don't need you to pay me back." He reached in his pocket and brought out a box. He opened it to show a ring. It was very simple, but probably not silver, even if it was that color, and it had a diamond in the middle, that seemed to sparkle with white fire. "Marry me, Helen."

Her voice went away again. She'd thought of all the reasons she shouldn't. People would say it was publicity. Her mom would say— She looked up and met his eyes, and like all those years ago, in the school hallway, she felt they belonged together. They'd always belonged together. "You can't possibly want to marry someone with the mind of an eighteen year old."

"It's not an eighteen year old. It's you. It's your mind." He was very serious. "And yes, I want to marry you. I was going to give you more time, but I don't want to. I waited so long—" He swallowed. "I know you have to be crazy to marry me. You'll start getting death threats from groupies tomorrow. And you'll need secretaries and body guards just to keep your privacy, but I love you Helen. And I want us to be married."

She felt her voice was lacking, again. When she found it, she said, "I don't care about all that, if I get time with you. If I get to be your wife."

"All the time you want. And that's what I want too. For you to be my wife. For me to be your husband. I don't care about anything else."

"Well, then, yes, I will marry you." Her voice felt hoarse and choked with tears, though she wasn't the slightest bit sad.

He leaned over and kissed her. And then she knew she really was awake.

The Magical Realm

E llen realized for the first time how much her husband had changed
when she took the tea into his office.

There is such a thing as the force of habit. One goes along, in life, and
life itself has a certain force and a certain pull. Ever since she'd married
Lir, she looked at him and saw the young man she'd once seen, coming
out of the waves, his skin glistening gold under the California moon. A
glance at the calendar told her it was thirty three years now since that
night, and that foolish young girl sitting on the soft sand, watching the
young men.

There were threads of white on Lir's hair now. Not many, but quite a
few. And traces of white on his well trimmed beard. There were wrinkles
at the corners of his green-blue oceanic eyes. Laughter wrinkles, mostly.
They'd had a good life, she thought.

But there was also a sadness, a listlessness, a look of distant and
unavoidable longing.

She went behind his shoulder and set the cup down at his right hand.
He looked up and smiled at her. His hands rested on the laptop keyboard,
but she couldn't help but see the document he had open was blank.
First page, first line and nothing on it. He'd taken a sabbatical from his
teaching job to write a book on little known myth. He'd been in the office
twelve ours a day for two weeks. But there was nothing on the page. And
he sat there with his longing look.

She'd had her doubts, many times, when they were first married.
Sometimes she caught a look in his eyes that made her wonder if

everything she'd done was justified. It had seemed so at the time, but young love as a way of deceiving everyone. Particularly those in love.

Later, when Murdoch and Muriann were born, she'd seen his delight in them. And he seemed so happy. But now, with Murdoch married and living across the country and Muriann away in London doing her post grad... He looked so tired. So very tired.

Instead of going out the door as she usually did after leaving him his herbal tea, designed to help him sleep, she slipped into a chair in front of the desk. He looked surprised, but smiled at her, his eyes crinkling.

"Is it being difficult?" she asked, striving for a light tone. "Your book?"

He smiled, and shrugged, as if to say it didn't matter. "Not precisely But for all these years, I thought it was the most important thing to do. I've studied so many of these obscure myths, kindled so many students' interest and curiosity in them, but... I don't know. I think it's depression." He hesitated. "I've been seeing a doctor."

"A doctor?" she asked, surprised. This was the man for whom she'd had to book every dental appointment and every checkup for years. It was as if the concept of doctors and illness had been completely foreign to him. She didn't pursue that thought.

"Well, a shrink, really," he said. "For about five years." He smiled at her surprise. "I didn't want it to hit you, or the kids. He prescribed some things, and at first it was .... It worked very well. It was like being young and full of fire, again. But lately—" He rubbed at his nose bridge. "Maybe I'm just getting old. I keep wondering who my parents were, and where I came from. At first, the whole.... not knowing anything about myself before the age of 17 was strange, but not.... not that strange. I built myself a life... we built ourselves a life. But now—"

"Yes," she said. "Yes." But she wasn't sure what she meant. She'd loved Lir from the first time she'd seen him, 33 years ago, under a September moon, coming out of the cold waters, the moonlight sparkling on his skin like magic dust.

She still loved him. She couldn't imagine life without him. But he looked tired, and old. And he'd been seeing a shrink, dosing himself with tablets. The wrongness of it made her wish to cry, but it was now too late for tears.

She lay in bed, staring at the ceiling, and got up before he did. At the break of day. She was fully dressed when he woke, and looked at her with wondering, sleep-fogged eyes. Then he reached for his glasses from the bedside and put them on. "You are fully dressed!" he said, and smiled teasingly. "So early!"

"I need to run an errand," she said, and came to the bed, and kissed him on the lips, lightly. She was going to miss this. "It is nothing much," she said. "I'll be back before lunch."

Before lunch... Her heart shrunk within her at the thought. But this was all wrong. Lir should not need glasses. He should not have wrinkles and gray hair. She did not mind them, but he did.

She must do what she had to do.

The people at the bank showed no surprise. Why should they? The safe deposit box had been paid for — had been paid for faithfully, every year — since they'd moved here twenty five years ago. She paid it in cash. Lir didn't even know about it. Almost the only secret she kept from him.

It had been her intention to leave him the key and a note, and she'd long since given his name and ID as an alternate. If she died, if anything happened to her, she wanted him to be able to reclaim his inheritance.

She hadn't thought she was selfish. Not really. She thought she'd die before him, and he'd go on to live his life, not the worse for the few years stolen from him.

But what if he died before her, in the high, dry reaches of Colorado, so far from all that was natural? No.

Steeling herself, she opened the box the solemn clerk handed her. It was one of the larger ones, in a vault filled with boxes, secret compartments. How many secrets were as odd and unbelievable as hers?

She opened it, took the bulky item, folded it carefully, feeling its silky folds, and put it reverently in a bag.

The box was now empty. There were no more secrets. Or there wouldn't be soon.

It was ten am when she got home, and the house was silent, the kitchen clean, Lir's juice glass rinsed and upside down by the sink.

SARAH A. HOYT

And it came to her she would miss that. Which was stupid. Well, there would be time for crying later.

He looked up as she came in the office, and spared a puzzled glass at her large bag.

She sat down on the chair. "I want to talk to you about the first time we met," she said.

He blinked at her. "At the college party?" she asked.

She shook her head. "No, before that."

"I don't remember meeting before that. Did we? Did I forget that? I'm sorry, I—"

"No, not your fault. It is mine. You see, when I was little, as you know, my parents had a house they rented every late summer and fall. By the sea, in California."

"Yes, I remember you—"

"Listen, please. You must let me tell this story."

He looked surprised at her unusual vehemence but inclined his head, in assent.

She took a deep breath. This was difficult enough. "When I was in high school, I wanted to be a marine biologist. So I was very happy when I realized a group of sea otters frolicked in the sea, near my parents' house. I went there to watch them, early morning, sometime in the evening. They are beautiful creatures and their antics made me happy.

"So one night I decided to watch them in the middle of the night. It was exactly 33 years ago last night. I slipped out to the beach, and I sat on a rock, and watched them. And then suddenly, the otters started taking off their pelts, while still in the water. Suddenly there was a group of young men, swimming and playing like children in the water, even though the water is very cold there. They didn't seem to mind. They were all in good shape, beautiful really—"

"My dear, if you're telling a Selkie story, you're telling it wrong. They're always female. And the animal they change into are seals, not otters. In fact, the conservation of mass—"

"No. Please listen. All of the young men were very beautiful, and I'd never watched a group of young men, not like that. They were all unself-conscious, and playing, really, like children, with no malice in them. None of the grown up stuff. They didn't see me, because I was up on the cliff, you know." She paused, and looked at him, and remembered how young and beautiful he had been. Would be. "One of them, to whom

58

they all deferred, was particularly handsome and powerful... I.... This is very hard to tell. I went back several times to watch him. Not them, him."

"I'm sure," he said, with mock gravity. "I can forgive your teen follies."

"Maybe you can," she said. "Wait till you hear them. Every time these young men came from the water, they took the pelts, and folded them, and put them each in a place."

"I'm sure you dreamed that part because—"

"Please, I don't know if I have the courage to continue, but here it goes. One night, after they came out of the water, I went down and took the pelt of the most handsome one. And I.... hid it. I made sure it was really hidden. I have no excuse. I just wanted him to stay. I wanted to look at him more." Lir frowned and she wasn't sure what he was thinking, but she went on, "And you know, I wanted to— Anyway. At sunrise, when the others went back to the sea, he stayed on the shore looking bewildered, and I was scared, so I ran home. After a while the local papers were full of a young man who'd wandered into town, mother naked and having no idea what his name was."

He opened his mouth, then closed it, thoughtfully.

"I kept track of you," she said, rushing, afraid of stopping, afraid of reason reasserting itself. "I kept track of you, as you .... well, you learn very fast, so you did high school in a year, and then I met you at college, and you know the rest."

He was frowning up at her. With the habit of decades, she could see him forming a joke, something to ease the tension. She could see he thought she'd gone insane. Before she lost courage, she stood up and pulled the glossy pelt from her bag and set it on his desk. "Here it is. You are free again. I should never have taken it. Magical creatures should never be forced to live and age in the world of mortals."

His expression had changed when he saw the pelt. All thought, all worry for her vanished from his face, and something like a light kindled in his eyes. He extended his hand and touched the pelt. Sparks flew, not fire but.... visible. Like tiny stars dancing around his hand. The longing in his eyes was unbearable.

She worried he'd put it on and shift right then and there. After all, they'd moved to Colorado, partly at her instigation, granted, to stop the possibility of his .... of his remembering? But if he shifted now, she'd have to drive most of a day with an otter in the car, to restore him home.

He didn't put it on or shift though. His eyes shone. His hair became dark again. The wrinkles disappeared. He smiled at her, a smile full of joy.

But enough remained of the human. He took his keys, his cellphone, his wallet. He held the pelt, walked around the desk, put it back in the bag. He hesitated for a moment, then bent and kissed the top of her head.

And then he rushed out. Out the door.

The house was very quiet. Very empty. It was like when the children moved out, first. Very silent, very empty. Almost like a house where someone had died. Which now she thought about it, was true. Lir, as she'd known him, was dead.

Oh, she hadn't thought of it, but she supposed she had to report him as a missing person, or the police would think she'd done away with him. As it was, they'd find his trail and the car, and they'd probably decide he'd disappeared on purpose.

It was going to be hard on the children, but it couldn't be helped. At least Lir would be happy again.

She cleaned the house that didn't need cleaning, and she thought about what she'd do with the rest of her life. Sure, she'd never become a marine biologist. And her business degree was quite rusty after years spent raising children. But maybe she could find something. They had savings. She could, at least, go back to school. Maybe study marine biology.

What she wouldn't do, what she couldn't do, was go back to that beach and watch the young men frolic in the waves.

The thought came that there were probably selkie females. Maybe he had someone waiting for him. She had a deep rooted conviction that they lived much longer lives than humans. What was 33 years out of eternity?

On the second day she organized their photos, started digitizing by scanning them into her computer. Maybe they'd bring some comfort to the kids, when the news came.

She didn't want to think of Lir, of where he was, of what he might be doing. Lir, as she'd known him had stopped existing. Perhaps he had forgotten his human life, just like the human had forgotten his magical life.

She'd decided she'd call in his disappearance after a week. Though depending on where the car was, she thought the police might call her first.

But she wanted to postpone the intrusion into their lives, and the inevitable shocked and pained phone calls from friends. And hurting the children.

It would have to be done. But she'd give it a week.

All of which would be easier if every time she closed her eyes at night, she didn't see young men frolicking in the waves under a golden moon, impervious to the cold air and colder water.

She moved through her days, like a shadow, feeling lost. The thing about a long-lasting marriage was that you stopped being just herself. They'd been Ellen and Lir. And now he was gone, and she felt as though one of her limbs, one of her essential parts had been amputated.

But she felt the phantom pain.

She woke up, without knowing she'd slept at all. There was a feeling she'd heard a door close, stealthily.

Someone had broken in.

She got up, put her glasses on, reached for her robe. The gun was still in the safe in the office. She—

There was a shadow in the doorway. A smell filled the room, one she associated with salt water and sun.

She blinked.

"I didn't mean to wake you, honey," Lir's voice said, very gentle.

"I— No. You—"

He walked towards the bed. He was carrying the bag, the same bag she'd given him and by the look of it with the pelt inside. He went into the closet, and came back out, without the bag.

He opened the dresser and took out his pajamas.

She was dreaming. She knew she was dreaming. She heard him shower and brush his teeth. After a while, he was in the doorway.

The light coming from the window shone on him, and she saw Lir.... Her Lir. There were white threads in his hair, and wrinkles at the corner of his eyes, and she had been there for each of those, for every moment that was marked on her face. He was wearing his glasses, which he took off and put on the bedside.

Her heart was hammering so hard she could hardly speak. "But I let you go," she said. "I gave you the pelt. I—"

He smiled. His hand — the left one, with the wedding band — reached across the bed to hold hers. His was a little cold. As though the coldness of the sea water lingered in it. Which was impossible of course. "I know," he said. "And thank you. I now know who I am, where I came from. I went back...." He closed his eyes. "It was...." He also seemed to have no words.

And she thought that it was kind, that it was like Lir to come back and say goodbye, to come back and try to leave her in a better place.

"I understand," she said. "I should never—"

"No, you listen. It is my turn to talk. It was lovely. Wonderful, really. And I remember many nights like that, sometimes frolicking with my people — all my people, of both sexes — on the edge between shore and sea. Many many nights. Hundreds of thousands of them. Frolicking in a state of innocence and happiness. You were right. I was a prince of the sea. I was.... oh, it's hard to explain."

"I know, you didn't need—"

"No, listen. Only I remembered our life too. Here, where the days change, where the years count. I remembered out life and our children, our happiness, our home. I remembered you." The hand holding hers squeezed. He bent, awkwardly, as if he hadn't done this thousands of times, and kissed her lips, gently. "And after two nights I grew restless. I wanted my magic, and my kingdom back."

"So, you're going back?" she said. "I know—"

His hand caressed her hair — which she knew also had white in it — and nestled in the curve of her shoulder, which had gotten rounded over the years. She knew an overweight middle aged housewife was nothing to the prince of the seas, but it was kind of him. So kind.

"I am back," he said. "I am back in my magic kingdom. The real one. I will never leave you. I could not. Leaving you hurt more than losing my pelt. You are my magic, Ellen."

Before she could find a word, or even get over her surprise, he kissed her.

His kiss tasted of the sea and moonlight.

And magic.

Wave

Hally happened to be at the registration desk when they came in, hand in hand, and for a moment she was fourteen again, and it somehow hurt as it had hurt back then. As if it were the most important thing in the world.

It was the summer that two dreams had died. One, that she'd get a swim team scholarship to college. And the other—

She used to have posters of him all over her room. Other girls had posters of rock stars, but she had Morgan Muir. Pictures of him smiling, lifting his Olympic gold medal aloft, when she was just seven or so.

Morgan Muir was when she'd first become aware that men were different, that she wanted to marry one someday. Well, beyond men being like daddy, of course. Not that she'd been exactly sure what the relationship between men and women was, just that you married a man and then he'd be with you all the time. Oh, and you got to wear a pretty white dress. And somehow babies appeared and they looked like him, and you got to be mom, and run the house.

By fourteen, she had a better idea. Enough to fuel daydreams. Not from the sex education classes. That whole thing was too real and vaguely squeaky. Dreaming about it would be like dreaming of butchering the chicken, instead of the Sunday roast all golden and mouth-watering. Instead her day dreams were composed of the love scenes in a million movies — not that she watched much, but when mom and dad were watching something, she caught glimpses of men and women embracing, their faces full of ecstasy of love, of belonging — and of stories of the

63

attraction between couples in books. Not that she read Romance because she simply wasn't that sort of girl. But there were love scenes in every adventure book, particularly westerns.

Sometimes in her daydreams he came and saved her, but more often she saved him, which is when he realized she was special and important and he loved her. This was because she was conscious of being ten years younger than him, and that the difference between fourteen and twenty one was a great gulf. She still looked like a little girl who'd grown too fast. She knew that. And he was a man.

But mostly the dreams were of how he'd smell like the salt sea, of the touch of his hand, of being held by him and told she was his one true love. Whatever feat of valor or devotion — a lot of the dreams involved arriving at his death bed, and somehow nursing him better — that got her there, the important thing was that she'd have him all for herself forever.

She'd never understood how he came to be where he was, though the papers later — with glossy photo montages and tales of how beautiful and romantic it was — had said something about a sail boat capsizing. But she'd learned long ago that newspapers just came up with some plausible story and ran with that. She remembered even the school newspaper had done that about the cookie sale for the swim team, saying the cookies were store bought and taken out of the package, when she'd just said that as a joke, and been at pains to describe the hours and hours of baking.

Besides sailing would be stupid unless he was really far off — and then how would he end up in her cove? — because the entire area had a ton of submerged rocks at high tide, the kind that you could only navigate if you'd grown up here and had the entire landscape in your head from years of familiarity.

She suspected he'd been climbing down the rocks to the cove and fallen. But perhaps he didn't want to say that to the paper, because it sounded stupid: great Olympic swimmer, slips and falls on wet seaside rocks, and almost kills himself.

However he came to the cove, she'd never have seen him if she hadn't come down early morning to practice. It was early March and mom and dad hadn't had the pool conditioned and open for the summer, at the hotel. And that was the other reason she headed for the cove. It wasn't that big. Just half the size of the pool. but it was surrounded by rocks which meant even as the tide came in, it was slightly warmer. Because the rocks gave off some of the warmth of the day, or something. Or perhaps it was an illusion. It just felt warmer.

She'd been early too, so the water was barely up to her ankles there. Not enough to swim. Which was good, because Morgan Muir — she'd paused, in her red swimsuit, the towel under her arm, sure she was dreaming — was in the cove, his mouth and nose only above water. Barely.

She'd tossed the towel, and scrambled down. With the tide coming in, he'd have been dead in minutes. If he wasn't dead already. He looked dead: pale as the belly of a fish, and limp as day-old catch.

She'd felt for his pulse, though, and there it was, beating at the side of his neck, in a regular thrum. And it was a good thing she felt for it, before she tried to lift him. Because when she tried to lift him, she could see half of his head was all over blood, which kept coming and coming, and mixing with the water.

Pressure. She thought, hazily from her high school first aid classes. Pressure.

First she tried to lift him, and when that didn't work, she'd gone and scrambled up the rocks, and got her towel. She got kind of under him, lifting his head out of water, and pushed the towel against the wound.

She still didn't quite remember how long she'd been in the pool. But it must have been two or three hours, because the tide came in completely, lifting them both, and she couldn't swim, not holding him above water, not with the towel now completely wet with his blood. Yes, she'd taken lifesaving, but she could never get a proper hold on him, while she had that towel pressed against his head. She kept thinking he should be dead, there was so much red on the towel. And she couldn't feel his pulse. There weren't enough hands.

The tide had kind of jammed her against one of the rocks, with her leg wedged against it, and she took advantage of that to keep his head above water.

Periodically, she called out, but the beach was pretty deserted till much later in the day. She didn't expect an answer. She kept wondering if she should or could hold him like this till there were people on the beach. Couldn't you die of hypothermia? Was he dead?

Suddenly, out of nowhere, it seemed, there were running steps on the beach, and she called out. Moments later a young woman stood on the rocks. She was Morgan's age, at least, and blond, and had on jogging pants and an old sweater.

She made a sound when she saw them, then plunged into the water, clothes and all, and relieved Hally of her burden.

Hally would never remember the conversation right, but it was all rushed. She thought the woman asked her if she had a cell phone. When she shook her head, the woman said, "Well, then, can you run and call 911 somewhere? I'll hold him up."

Hally felt half dead, but she scrambled up, and ran stumbling to the stairs that went all the way up to clifftop, the hotel her parents owned and managed.

And then she didn't remember anything. Mom said she'd come in and said "Morgan Muir is dying in the cove where I swim, in the beach. Call 911." And collapsed.

Turned out the leg she'd wedged on the rock was cut almost to the bone.

"I have no idea how you managed to run on that leg," was what she remembered the doctor saying when she'd woken in the hospital, recovering from blood loss and pneumonia.

She hadn't said anything, because a hellish throat infection had piled on the pneumonia, and she couldn't talk.

The pneumonia had been bad. Really bad. She'd spent ten days in the hospital on IV antibiotics.

That was when she had first become aware of Kemp. Kemp had been in swim team with her forever, but apparently he was volunteering at the hospital that summer. And also, he looked completely different from during the school year. Like he'd grown a foot, being now taller than her, and his voice had dropped.

The first time he'd seen her, he'd just smiled and said hi. But then he kept coming back, with flowers, and books — he'd bought her the ridiculously expensive, illustrated fairy tale book she'd been mooning over in the local bookshop — and hard candy which made her throat feel better.

It was funny because in her head she remembered that time as two different things. One was getting to know Kemp, and thinking what a great guy he was to be paying so much attention to her.

Another was lying in the hospital bed, knowing she'd be out of shape for swim team, and — when the infection set in on her leg and they told her the bone itself had been cut, and that she might never walk without a limp — that she'd probably never get the scholarship she'd been aiming for, and never get to go off and study art. Lying in the hospital and reading the newspapers and magazines about how Morgan Muir's fiancée had saved his life, and how romantic it was, and how the wedding was planned for the next month, and all the celebrities who'd be attending.

No wonder the nurses kept giving her sleeping pills. She didn't take them, but practiced sleight of hand and then hid them in the box of pencils mom had brought her from home. She didn't like taking tablets was all.

But it had led to the temptation.

On her tenth day in the hospital, when she had been waiting for the doctor to come in and discharge her, Morgan and Marissa, his fiancée, had come in. They were all put together, and she looked perfect, make up and designer jeans and all.

Hally could talk now, but found that in their presence she couldn't find her voice.

"I hear you saved me," Morgan said. "And you got sick because of it. I'm sorry."

His voice in person was oddly disconcerting. It sounded more mundane than when she heard him in interviews. Like it had less resonance.

He and Marissa had brought in coffee, from the drive-through place that was expensive, and they'd got her a hot chocolate. "Your mom said you like that."

She'd sat there and sipped, and then the nurse came in. And of course, she fawned all over Morgan and Marissa. Because "so romantic."

They'd left their coffees on the tray by the bed, and she'd thought—

For just a moment she thought she could put the tablets into Marissa's cup. There were nine. It would probably kill her. And no one knew she had them. And it could be some big accident.

But then she heard, in her mind, clear as day "No. You're meant for better things."

And that was it. It was like a thought, but not her thought. And she blinked in shock. What better things? What could be better than consoling Morgan. Having Morgan fall in love with her.

Only—

Only she'd know she killed someone. Even if he fell in love with her — as if there were no other women in the world — she couldn't live with it. She couldn't.

She sipped hot chocolate, and Morgan and Marissa talked to the nurses, and Kemp put his head in, with a big smile, "Still waiting for discharge, Hally? I'll go grab Doctor Grant."

And now, now twenty years later, here were Morgan and Marissa coming into her hotel to register for a stay. She guessed Kemp must have taken the reservation, because she'd have noticed the name.

She smiled at them, as she registered them, and gave them the room key. Her parents had retired and left her and Kemp in charge of the hotel ten years ago. After she'd finished her art degree. Which she mostly used to make haunting drawings of mermaids and knights. They sold really well in the gift shop.

Morgan's hair was receding. Marissa seemed to wear more makeup than Hally remembered. But they looked happy.

As she was signing them in, Morgan looked at her name tag. "Halcyone! Like the girl who—" He paused, and his face split in a big grin. Suddenly he was pumping her hand, saying "You saved my life. Marissa told me."

"Oh, it was nothing," Hally said, and just then Kemp came in, saying something about pool maintenance.

The four of them ended up having dinner together that night, after Kemp and Hally lined up a babysitter for their kids. "The twelve-year-old," Kemp explained. "Could babysit them all, but you know what the law is, so we get a babysitter."

"I remember those days," Marina said, her voice reminiscent. "The twins are away at college, though."

During dinner, Hally kept trying to figure out what had been so special about Morgan; what caused that terrible ache of her 14th summer. He was a nice, middle aged man, with receding blond hair, and a devoted wife.

She didn't regret getting injured saving him. He and Marissa seemed very happy. And somehow, that summer, she'd got Kemp.

As if knowing what she was thinking, he reached and caught her hand, under the table. His hand was very warm, very firm.

And his hold on life and love and the future would never let her drown.

Wild Hair

I t wasn't like her to have a wild hair day. It simply wasn't.

Rahel had been a compliant child and was a well-behaved adult. And if sometimes she was a little impatient with herself, if she felt lonely or locked into a life that was predictable and ordered and dutiful, at least she was safe.

Being safe had been her goal since she was very young, and since mom had told her what happened. And what her father had been.

So, the last thing she expected herself to do was dye her hair a strange and artificial gold. And she'd never be able to explain it. It was, she supposed, a combination of things. For one, two days before, she'd found a white hair amid her mousy brown mane. Not that it mattered. Why should it matter? She supposed at 28 she was not so young. Women in the middle ages would be dead by her time of life, right?

But the white hair had bothered her. Like it was unfair. White hairs should come when one had lived a long life and done a lot of things, not when all one had done was study and work, live at home, and then in a very clean apartment in the big city.

So, she'd put her hair up, as she always did, and pinned it, but it seemed to her like it screamed for attention from the mirror.

It didn't, of course, and even if her hair went white overnight, like Marie Antoinette's was said to have, it didn't matter, because she worked from home. She'd moved to the city mostly .... well, mostly because it was easier to be alone and to keep to herself in the city than to be alone and keep to herself in the small town, she'd grown up in.

If what mom had said was right, sooner or later, people back at home would notice. They had already noticed that she had stopped dating in 10th grade and distanced herself from all her friends.

No one noticed in the city. The neighbors probably wouldn't even notice if she dropped dead. Part of the reason she didn't even have a cat — besides the fact she was afraid she'd go weird and turn the cat into a frog or something — was that she didn't want her cat to eat her, which seemed to be the inevitable conclusion of someone who lived alone dying. As was, she wasn't absolutely sure that fate or luck or something wouldn't conjure up a cat out of nowhere to eat her, should she die in her 22nd floor apartment.

And perhaps that too was part of the reason she'd bought the hair dye. After a long day of scientific translation — it paid well, and it was easy, but it didn't do much for those parts of her mind that weren't fully rational and logic — and catching glimpses of that bright white hair in her reflection on the window, she'd gone to the grocery store for food. Because, of course, she'd run out of food that day. The heat-and-eat dinners that she bought by the month-supply and of which she was supposed to have ten left had mysteriously vanished, leaving her freezer empty.

She glared at the empty freezer for a while, then put on jeans and a sweatshirt and ran to the grocery store two blocks away. Really ran, because the weather had turned unexpectedly cold. Well, maybe not unexpectedly, since it was Denver, and it was October. But it had been in the seventies last time she'd been out of the house, and now it was .... felt like twenties.

She ran all the way, thinking she'd come out and buy a proper amount later. She'd just grab frozen pizza or something.

And on the way to the frozen pizza — rushing across the store amid couples shopping with their kids, and singles who seemed to be eyeing each other more than the food, she found herself, inexplicably, in the hair dye isle, and staring at a box that promised "Metallic golden sheen."

How the box happened to be in the bag with the frozen pizza by the time she got home, she'd never be fully able to explain. But while the pizza was baking, she thought, well, if she was going to have white hairs soon, shouldn't she have really extraordinary golden hair? Just once in her life?

And after eating half the pizza — it wasn't very big — she found herself in her tiny bathroom, fooling around with malodorous chemicals, and an hour and a half later her hair was gold. No, really gold, like it had been spun from pyrite, which always seemed more gold than real gold.

She stared at herself, in the mirror, mouth half-open. It wasn't that it was ugly, precisely. What it was, wasn't natural. And it certainly wasn't .... right. Not for Rahel. She'd always been the sort of girl who tied her hair back, who didn't wear makeup, who didn't call attention to herself.

Because after all, anyone who got close, other than mom, might notice she wasn't quite human.

Now she had a golden mane, sparkling and catching the light, and it made her small, pale face look smaller and paler.

She glared at herself in the mirror, and tied her hair back, as she always did, and went to bed.

There was a storm, during the night. Nothing surprising there, of course. It was Colorado, and it was fall. But as she woke up in the morning, she could swear she heard, amid the howling of the wind, and the tap-tap of the snow and hail against her window, a voice crying out, very faintly "Rahel, Rahel, throw down your golden hair."

This both made her giggle and annoyed her. She didn't like fairy tales, anyway. And of all the fairy tales she despised Rapunzel the most. Partly because it was so insanely non-sensical. What kind of person would let anyone — let alone a full-grown man — climb up an endless tower on their hair? It would hurt.

She ate a cold slice of pizza for breakfast and washed it down with tea. With the cold outside, she didn't even bother dressing. She wasn't going anywhere today. Instead, she put a robe on over her fluffy slippers and sat down to finish the research on a new kind of ceramic that she was translating from German to English.

As the night started falling, she heard it again — even though the wind had gone quiet — "Rahel, Rahel, throw down your golden hair."

She went to the window, then, and looked down her building. Which wasn't exactly easy to do. It had to be done sideways and at an angle, since of course, she couldn't look straight down.

The snow was still falling, and with the streetlights sparkling on it, it was hard to actually see anything very clearly, but she was sure — she would always be sure — that there was a man, climbing up the glass wall, looking much like a cartoon spiderman. Except that he wasn't wearing the suit and that — she swore — he waved up at her. Even though he must be 10 floors down.

She frowned at him and closed the curtains. She had the rest of the pizza for dinner, and then went to bed.

The morning was calmer, still cold looking, and she woke up to a voice, now more distinct "Rahel, Rahel, throw down your golden hair."

Well, okay, it was probably hallucinations, because she hadn't eaten in much too long. Or she hadn't eaten anything but pizza. Not that this was unusual. But obviously as you got old enough to have white hairs, you couldn't skip meals.

She showered and dressed, and put her hair up, but it didn't look right. That mass of golden hair, and her small, pale face.

She looked through the drawers thinking she might have some blush from when she'd come to town for the interview. She didn't really like makeup, and she didn't think she looked particularly good in it — it tended to look ridiculous and artificial — so she was surprised to find she had not a little box of blush, but a full make up kit. Thinking about it, she could dimly remember having bought it because she was in a hurry and it was the only thing available at the store where she'd stopped.

Tentatively she applied blush and was surprised because it looked natural. Really natural. Just better, so that ... well, it went with the hair. Next thing she knew, she'd applied eyeshadow and mascara and some lipstick, though really, it was more like lip gloss.

She glared at herself in the mirror, because it didn't look like her. It didn't look bad, though. Just like a complete stranger.

She grabbed her winter coat from the closet, but didn't pull up the hood, and as she walked to the grocery store, she saw that the diner she usually passed at a run was only half full — not full to the door as it usually was — and thought: why not?

Part of it might have been the smell of breakfast and the fact that she was really, really hungry.

Sitting at the table, in the corner, she ordered breakfast, and wished she'd brought a book. That's what she usually did on the rare occasions she ate out. She brought a book, and read it, and that kept people from approaching her.

But she'd forgotten to bring a book, which is why she looked around and realized there was someone staring at her. He was tall and dark, and blunt featured. And he was holding a book in his hand, but he was staring at her like he'd never seen a woman before.

She knew she'd put the makeup on all wrong or something. She probably looked ridiculous.

Just then her eggs and pancakes arrived, and she ate in a hurry, then got to the supermarket and bought — rather blindly — some fruit and bread, and a dozen eggs and some milk.

By the time she got to the apartment, her phone started ringing in her pocket.

I was mom and Rahel talked to her, while putting things away. "No, mom," she said, as she'd been saying every week, for a year. "I'm not seeing anyone. I promise I won't. And no, I haven't turned anyone into a frog by accident."

Mom squawked on the other side that she'd said nothing about turning people into frogs, and that she never said anything about that nonsense magic, and that—

But the truth was that it was little more than what she said. All about dad's amazing, near-supernatural attractiveness to the opposite sex, and how he couldn't help being the way he was because he was so stunningly beautiful, and had something near irresistible, and how Rahel needed to be careful, because she'd likely inherited it.

Mom was still saying it, of course, "You know, it's just I don't want you to end up having relationships with people and breaking their hearts, and promising more than you can give, and—"

It was the old sermon all over again, first brought up and unrolled when she'd been dating Bobby in tenth grade.

"Oh, Bobby Smith," mom said, suddenly out of the blue. "Remember him?" And interpreting Rahel's mumble as assent. "His wife just had their third kid."

Just for that, because she felt inexplicably resentful, but also because frankly she didn't want to put up with another sermon, Rahel didn't tell mom about the hair and makeup.

Instead, she worked and had some dinner, and spent some time in front of the mirror brushing her golden hair, before going to bed. The weird thing was even after she washed her face, she still looked like the golden hair belonged. Maybe that was all the young man in the diner had been looking at.

She was reading a very boring — well recommended — book before bed when she heard it, clearer and much nearer "Rahel, Rahel, throw down your golden hair!"

She ran to the window and threw open the curtains, and he was there. And he couldn't be there because it made no sense. Men do not climb the glass faces of buildings to knock at the window of single ladies, just because they saw them a few tables away, in the diner.

But he was there, knocking at the window, with a big grin on his face, and she could see his lips form the words, "Rahel, Rahel, throw down your golden hair."

She closed the curtains, ran to the bed, and sat huddled, trying to figure out if she should call 911. But what would she tell them? "Some guy climbed my building and is outside the window of the twenty second floor?" They'd think she was doing drugs.

She went to the window again and peered around the curtain. And of course, there was no one there. She must have dreamed it. But the snow had picked up again, and it howled outside.

She sighed. Well, at least she had food. But she had trouble sleeping that night. Everything kept coming back to her, and suddenly, as if she'd both always known it, and it were a new and startling idea, realized that she was lonely. Very lonely.

Dad had left when she was what? Four? Five? And she'd never really bonded with mom.

Mom wasn't mean or cruel, or anything like that. Rahel figured out early on, mom was just hurt. She'd been really upset when dad had left like that. It was all part of living in a small town. Dad had blown in out of nowhere, and mom had married him, and then he'd disappeared. And everyone in town said she should have known better than marrying a stranger.

Mom said he'd left her for another woman. That he'd had affairs all the time they'd been married. And that it was because he was so fatally attractive. She said Rahel was too — though Rahel had never seen it in herself — and that she shouldn't trifle with young men, because she couldn't be faithful, and it was better not to break anyone's heart.

Which was why Rahel had broken up with Bobby. Good Lord, they'd never even kissed. Just held hands and talked about books.

She realized she very much wanted someone to hold hands and talk about books. Was that so terrible? Was it because she was too much like dad?

In the morning, she had time. The job she'd been doing was ahead of schedule, because she'd been working late — probably because the current book was really tiresome — and she thought she'd look up dad's name, see if she could find pictures.

She did. Online. Not recent pictures, but some pictures of himself as a young man — though he was online even now. Or at least she found a fakebook account with the same name — and she did not look like him at all. If anything, she looked like mom. Not that she looked a lot like mom.

As a young man, dad looked like.... Well, his name was Earnest Prinz. And he looked like the Disney version of a fairytale prince. Though the hair was not quite as dorky. He was blue eyed, and had golden hair, and the broad shoulders and narrow waist of a cartoon character.

Looking at the pictures, she thought she heard a knocking on her window and the distant calling "Rahel, Rahel, throw down your golden hair" but ignored it.

Instead, she friended her dad on Facebook, which required of course making an account. And sent him a message saying "I know you probably don't even remember me—"

She got back an answer before she was done typing, "Rahel! Is it really you?"

A quick exchange of texts. He swore he didn't know she was even alive. He'd looked for her. He'd even hired a detective. But they couldn't find her, and mom had told him Rahel had died.

There were strange things in what he said. Almost as weird as mom's. Like his saying that he might not have hired the best detective, "Because I'm not sure about those things in your world." And also "It wouldn't be weird if you'd died, because you know, our kind sometimes does, there."

But he'd said he had made the Facebook account simply to talk to her, and that if she just waited, he'd come and see her.

"You live in Denver?" she asked.

"No, but I can be there in minutes."

Because she wasn't sure — yes, he was her father, but he was also a stranger — she arranged to meet him at the botanic gardens, despite the snow.

She didn't even mind the snow that much, as she stood in the deserted Japanese gardens and saw him approach. There was something strange about his attire, like he was trying to look mundane, but couldn't quite manage it. His clothes looked.... too new, his hair too perfect. Maybe that was all mom meant.

"You look like your grandmother Titania," he said.

"My grandmother's name was Titania? Maybe I can turn people to frogs."

He smiled uneasily. After a while he asked what her mother had told her about him, about herself.

"We are magical, Rahel. Your mom was afraid of it. She was afraid the magic would manifest. You see, this is not the only world. There is a place... You can call it fairyland if it makes you feel better." The story was fantastic, unimaginable. "I should never have married your mother. But I fell in love with her. And then she .... she couldn't accept it. And I wasn't very good at this world. There aren't many jobs for elf-prince. Well, maybe movies, but that's not the point."

Rahel would like to think he was insane. But the thing was, dad — and she was sure he was dad — wasn't young, but he wasn't old. There was this feeling of eternity around him.

"But I'm not like you," Rahel said. "I'm just human. I had a white hair!"

"I think you made yourself have white hairs. No, I'm not going to argue. I know it's hard for people like you to believe in fairyland. But you need to be who you are. You're at odds with the world because you don't let yourself be who you are."

He didn't ask to meet her again, though he said anytime. And Rahel went back home, sure it was all insane.

Later, she stood in front of the mirror and thought about letting herself be who she really was. How did one even do that? But she could feel as if there had been.... something over her thoughts, something heavy.

Perhaps dad was right. Or perhaps he was just crazy. Not that mom was particularly sane either. But perhaps it was time to be herself, and not who her parents said she was.

It seemed to her, suddenly, she looked quite different.

She brushed her hair, and tied it back, and then she thought she'd send dad a picture of the hair dye box, so she could show him it was just dye. Because he kept saying her hair was just like her grandmother Titania's.

The thing was the box had disappeared. I was completely gone. Not in the bathroom trash, and not in the kitchen trash, and she hadn't taken it out, and she didn't have a cleaning service.

She did some work, and went to bed. As she was falling asleep, someone knocked at the door. Which was strange because she had a doorbell. Weirder, as she reached for the light switch, nothing happened.

She put on a robe and went to the door, and there, looking worried, was the young man from the diner. "Hi, I'm John. I live next door. Something blew in the building, and they're trying to figure out which apartment caused it."

She'd never have let him in, of course, but there were other men, and they had IDs from the electric company, and anyway the hallways were full of people looking around, people she remembered seeing before.

They found the short, eventually. The lights up on the roof terrace had blown. Probably too much snow, the guys said.

And John had seen her back to her apartment, and stood, and cleared his throat, "Would you— You wouldn't—That is.... breakfast? Tomorrow?"

They'd had breakfast, and then other breakfasts. And they'd held hands and gone to the movies and talked about books.

Eventually he'd asked if it wouldn't be a good idea if they got married, and she tried to explain what mother had told her, and what father had told her. And he hadn't laughed. He hadn't called a psychiatrist. He'd held her hand and said, "To me you are magical. And that's a good thing."

Her hair never went back to mousy brown. In fact, she couldn't find a picture of herself with mousy brown hair, and all the kids — three boys and two girls — had the same bright gold hair.

And she could never find her dad's account on Facebook, again. A year after being married, she got a text with his name that said, "you made your choice."

And she had. Mother came around eventually and stopped giving Rahel that strange look, like she expected Rahel to turn people into frogs. And she never gave it to the kids.

John always said Rahel was magical, but he didn't seem to see anything wrong with that.

Her hair did, eventually, go white. But it didn't matter at all, when John held her in his arms and whispered in her ear, "Rahel, Rahel, let down your golden hair."

Magic Mirror

W hat on Earth do you do with a magic mirror?

Ellie Jones turned the thing over and over in her hand, in some confusion. It was silver, and it had handle, but the size was like those stupid hand mirrors that women used to carry in their purses back when *I need to go powder my nose* was a thing.

The silver was tarnished and the elaborate scroll work on back and handle spoke of something very old. Not that Ellie was an expert. She was an accountant, not an art major. But it seemed to her this was older than most "antiques" she'd come across which were, at most, Victorian. And they looked subtly alien, like nothing she'd ever run across before.

At the very back, center, there was a clear space that might one day have held initials, but nothing but the vaguest tracery showed, and it was impossible to imagine what those initials might have been. For one, they didn't fit in with the normal alphabet.

But possibly the most puzzling and strangest thing of all was the note with the mirror.

To begin with it was in Ellie's mother's hand as it used to be. And Ellie's mother was 65, and since dad died her handwriting had got spidery and odd. So, mom didn't write anything by hand if she could help it.

Ellie would have understood better if this had been a typed note with a signature at the bottom. Not that it made the contents any easier to make sense of. Not for the first time, Ellie thought she needed to make time to go see mom. But she'd been so slammed with work... Still, this letter spoke of some kind of brain issue, and the soonest she could evaluate her mom's functioning the better.

Mom was all alone in nowheresvillle Ohio, and all her friends had moved away to warmer climates, and then dad had died, and mom was cleaning the house — she said — to put up for sale really soon. Only soon never came.

Her parents had been pack rats, and as far as she could tell so had every ancestor going back to Ira Jones who had built the house as a farmhouse in what was back then an advanced settlement in the wild west that Ohio was at the time.

And through Indian raids, and colonization moving way past them, the Jones had stayed in their old farmhouse, fixing, and enlarging as times and need dictated, and selling their land parcel by parcel, until they were sitting on the main street of Janus, Ohio, one of those cities you could miss entirely by blinking. It had a drug store, two restaurants — a pizza house and a diner — a tiny grocery store that sold mostly local produce in season, a school where all grades went and where the graduating class was usually under fifty students, and a library. Oh, they also had a traffic light, right on the corner with the library, the school, and the two restaurants. People were right proud of that streetlight, even though it was rarely needed and the old ladies who constituted the highest demographic in Janus ignored it routinely.

It had, however, occurred to Ellie that given the family proclivities and how stuffed every room in their place was, from unused rooms up to the attics and what had once been the barn and had been converted into a garage and workshop with its own attic over those, cleaning the house to sell might be akin to the work of Hercules clearing the Augean stables.

It had obviously started affecting mom because the note read:

Dear daughter,

I found this in the attic. It is a magic mirror. I have a very vague memory of your dad telling me his grandmother told him it belonged to some ancestress in Europe who was royal, or perhaps a king's mistress, and that the magic mirror accounted for how all his ancestresses were so successful and had such happy lives.

I am not absolutely sure what to do with it, and at any rate, it only works with women of the Jones line, which I, of course, am not. So I'm sending it to you, and I hope it works for you.

Love,

Mom

Ellie's first impulse was to be mad at mom. Because Ellie was perfectly happy and successful and didn't need a magic mirror.

Oh, okay, so her career was not glamorous, but she'd never had the slightest interest in being glamorous, or in having some career in the movies, or dancing or whatever. Yes, she'd heard her ancestresses, on dad's side, had done all that but ever since Ellie had been old enough to evaluate herself, she hadn't needed a magic mirror to tell her she was plain. Not ugly. Ugly might have been better. In the few parties she'd attended, in the achingly awkward years of high school and college, she'd seen ugly women with hook noses, too large mouths, or just ugly looking, who'd held men spell bound because they acted as if they were gorgeous. There was power in being that ugly. The eye was attracted and stayed, despite itself. And if the woman then could say something entertaining, or display intelligence, men would fall over themselves to be near her.

But Ellie Jones was plain. She had a face in shape of a face, brown eyes in the shape of eyes, lips a little too straight and thin, but nothing out of the ordinary way. After her junior year in college, she'd stopped wearing makeup, because it did nothing for her. She had a plain, round, kindly face that some farmer in Janus in the nineteenth century might very well think he might as well take to wife, because she wasn't hard to look at. But in the twenty first century men had more choices, and at any rate saw what real beauty looked like in commercials and movies and TV. And none of them had looked at her twice, unless they needed help with their homework, or something.

And so, having evaluate her assets and deciding her greatest one was her ability with numbers, though not for higher math, Ellie had charted a course for accountancy, graduated with top grades, and now worked for a large engineering firm in Denver Colorado, and had made enough to buy a little house in the suburbs. She had her house, her lawn, her tidy little kitchen.

Truly, she only felt unhappy when the snow was piling high outside, and she couldn't go out to work, or out to dinner somewhere. She'd long ago found the answer to what you do when you go out to eat alone at a nice sit-down restaurant: you take a book. She could sit through a candlelight meal with herself and enjoy the fact there were people around her without in the least needing to engage with them. And the couples having dinner in those restaurants might look deliriously happy, but she would bet they still had fights about whose turn it was to do the dishes.

She was perfectly happy. At twenty-nine, the pictures of happy families in her erstwhile classmates Christmas cards didn't make her question her path in life. She'd never thought she could have what they did, so she found no cause to repine. She was saving for retirement, and she would have a comfortable old age.

Indeed, the only thing making her unhappy was this strange mirror and the idea that her mom, maybe, thought she was unhappy.

She sat on the bed, where she'd sat to open the mail, and turned the mirror over and over in her hands. She raised it to look at herself. And yep, she looked as she had always done. Feeling stupid, in her strictly utilitarian bedroom lit by the light of the setting sun, she spoke to the mirror, "Mirror mirror... on my hand, who's the fairest of the .... band?"

Nothing happened of course. Well, almost nothing, except that from the depths of the mirror it seemed to her she heard a snort of laughter. Which she was almost sure she'd imagined.

She put the mirror and the pile of bills and offers for retirement seminars — really, at what age did they think people retired? — on top of her dresser to tidy up later, and went to the kitchen, to warm up the leftovers of the last restaurant meal.

And then she went to bed. And had the strangest dreams, in which she was a king's mistress. Or perhaps his pre-mistress.

She was still herself, Ellie Jones, plain as bread and twice as wholesome, decked out in belle-epoque attire. But of all the women in the court, the king was fascinated with her. And all the women envied her and hated her. And there were rumors that he meant to defy the marriage arranged for him since he was three and marry her.

And every night, she brought out that same mirror and looked into it, and said, "Not by hook and not by crook, and not by a love spell, but bring me my perfect husband, and make him see my true beauty, so we might in love dwell."

When Ellie woke up, her first thought was that it was execrable poetry. But there was a feeling that it was a translation, not even from one language but many, as languages had changed over the existence of the mirror. Which was silly. There hadn't even been any glass mirrors until the seventeenth century. Or at least she was sure she had seen that in the Treasures of the Louvre exhibit in the Denver Art Museum last month.

She looked at the silver handle protruding from the colorful circulars on the dresser and grinned ruefully to herself. All right, then. Grabbing the mirror, she spoke the words to it, and just about managed not to giggle as she said them.

From deep within the mirror — this time she was sure — there was a sigh, like a gust of wind. She put it down and showered and dressed and went to work.

At the end of the day, more or less on a whim, she thought she'd go to the art museum and go through the exhibit again. At least it saved her going home and looking at the mirror again. It was a silly thing. She should call mom.

But instead, she went to the museum, which was deserted in the last two hours before closing. And she did what she always did, walking solemnly through the exhibits, reading the cards. She was staring in some awe at the little chair completely covered in gold leaf, when someone said behind her, "Seems like it would be terribly uncomfortable, doesn't it?"

She turned around and or a moment was confused because this man looked exactly like the king in her dream. Which actually meant he wasn't precisely handsome. He had strong features and expressive eyes and unlike the king, he was older than Ellie. Probably forty or forty-five, with a touch of grey at the temples. Also, Ellie knew him. Or rather knew him by sight, though she'd never had any occasion to work with him. He was one of the chief engineers on the big aviation project. She looked over her shoulder and said, "I'm sorry. I don't remember your name. And yes, the chair looks like it would hurt your back if you sit in it too long. But I think they were smaller people than we are."

He grinned. "Undoubtedly. And not as spoiled. I like being spoiled. My name is Clay. Clay Wolf. And you are.... Helen? Jones."

"Ellie. In the accounting department."

He smiled, and just like the king in her dream, he had a thousand-watt smile, "I thought it was something like that. I have a horrible memory for names, though." His grin became self-conscious, "You come to museums often?"

She shrugged and felt herself blush as the admission seemed stupid. "I live alone," she said.

"Yeah, me too. Well. My wife died years ago and I... It's easier to be alone, you know. But sometimes I get bored."

They went through the rest of the exhibit together. He had a subtle sense of humor, but mostly he was just comfortable to be around. When he asked Ellie to dinner it didn't seem like he was on the make, or like he was hitting on her because she was plain so she must be easy. It just seemed like he wanted to go to dinner with her.

They went to a little steakhouse self-consciously styled as ye old tavern. The food was good, but more importantly, they'd fallen into talking about books. They were both mystery fans, who had cut their teeth on Agatha Christie.

"My mom said literally," Clay said with a laugh. "I ruined her leather-bound collection."

It had been comfortable, and companionable, and not demanding. And Ellie really hadn't expected to see or hear from him again, except for waving, by chance, in the hallways.

But that night, not sure what possessed her, she said the words while looking at the mirror again. And from its depths came a sigh.

Next morning, Clay stopped by her desk to bring her mystery he'd just finished and which he thought she'd like.

That weekend he asked her out to the natural history museum. She'd gone a million times, but she liked dinosaurs, so she said yes. Afterwards, they walked around the lake in City Park and talked about mysteries, and about completely mundane things, like lawn care, and how to build what looked like a traditional library from shelves from Ikea.

Turned out he lived a few streets from her, in the same development, in a slightly larger house.

At work, they fell into the habit of eating lunch together because they always had something to talk about. And they did things together on the weekend, and it was always fun.

And even though he kissed her one weekend, Ellie still expected nothing from this but a close friendship. Clay had told her about his wife, who had been his high school sweetheart, and shown her pictures. Jane Wolf had been a beautiful woman, and Clay said, "After her, no one seemed right, and the idea of dating was dreary." Ellie could see why, and she expected nothing.

But every night she said the words to the mirror. And she still hadn't called her mom.

Three months later, when the snow was just starting to fall, and they sat on a bench in city park, letting it dust their coats and hats, Clay had asked Ellie to marry him.

It had been strangely romantic. He'd said "I've been looking for very long for someone to be the companion of my heart. But I didn't even know how to get to know someone. Now I know you, Ellie, and I know you're my perfect match, and if you're willing to marry an old and stodgy man, you'll make me very happy."

For some reason Ellie still didn't call her mom, until they'd got married, just the two of them and two — bewildered looking — co-workers as witnesses in a civil registry office a week later.

Ellie went into the house to pack her clothes, as they'd decided they'd live in his, larger house and sell hers, and saw the mirror. And realized how odd it was that she still hadn't called her mom.

Mom sounded absolutely normal on the phone, and only slightly shocked at the news. She seemed however completely willing to forgive Ellie's lapse, Ellie guessed because she could already hear the pitty-patter of little grandchildren feet. As she remembered her own grandmother saying, the grandmother clock was the most unforgiving clock of all because you couldn't really do anything about it, not if you were a decent human.

It wasn't until she mentioned the mirror that mom sounded startled. "Oh, no, Ellie. I didn't write that. The letter was in the box with it when I found it, and I thought you'd like it, since you always like museums and stuff. Of course, the magic thing is nonsense, but it's an antique and I thought you might appreciate it."

There was a long silence because Ellie couldn't think what to say. She finally said, "I appreciate it very much indeed."

Months later, while pregnant with her first child, while they cleaned out her house to put on the market, she packed the mirror away carefully.

Who knew? Someday she might have a daughter or a grand daughter who would need the mirror to find the courage to look for a full life, even if she wasn't the most beautiful of them all. Or of the band.

As she closed the box and put it in a box of keepsakes to go into the attic of their house, she thought she heard a distant giggle, as if from the depths of a magic mirror.

Hoard

Noah Forest wasn't ready for the wave of nostalgia that washed over him as he drove into the old hometown.

He had no real use for nostalgia, and one of his biggest problems with Natalie had been how she used to mainline Hallmark movies, all with the same plot: girl from small town goes back home after disappointment in big city and finds herself falling n love with the little town and the man she left behind. This habit was all the more annoying since Natalie had never, once, in her life spent more time in a small town than perhaps required to grab a meal on a long interstate trip. And not much of that. Natalie preferred flying. Particularly private flights.

Noah was not a woman; he'd been very happy to leave the small town behind; he hadn't been disappointed by the big city; and frankly he was only coming back to take care of paperwork and to sell the farm.

Why his dad had insisted on staying behind, in Colorado, and persist on farming the same old plot of land, which wouldn't be fertile barring Colorado exchanging climate with North Carolina, he didn't know. Sure, it had been his grandparents' home and his great grandparents before that, and the family had roots deep in the rocky and arid soil of Silver Ridge as far back as there had been English speakers here and judging by the number of brides who appeared in the family records and the family's ability to tan, probably a good deal longer. But the land was no good, and it had never managed to keep the family much above subsistence level and even modern machinery hadn't managed to make much of it.

What the damnfool woman with buying it, he didn't know. He didn't care, either. He just wanted the 200 acres of rocks and blowing dust, with occasional tumble weeds and brief interruptions of snow and ice out of his hands, and out of his mind.

Then he could go back to New York and his real life.

Of course, Silver Ridge being where – as dad used to say with a chuckle – Judas had lost his boots, there was no way to fly directly there. Or perhaps there was. There had been some kind of private airport, hadn't there? Someone... One of the nearby farmers had a landing field? He remembered something from a conversation with Dad, long ago, before the stroke had made Dad's speech too slurred to understand over the phone.

But Noah couldn't remember exactly who had the field, or where it was, or how to charter a flight of the right size to get there. Of course, all that, probably, could have been handled by his secretary.

But the crazy woman who wanted to buy the farm – he had an image of her in his head, as this wild-haired hippie in flowing, embroidered skirts, and probably reeking of pot a mile away – had insisted she wanted to close the week before Christmas, which had given him three days to get everything done. Even if Jennie was a wonder and a miracle as a secretary, you really couldn't ask her to drop everything and get him flights to Silver Ridge. Well, and even if you could, it was entirely possible that there were no flights, but by the time he found that out, he'd not have left himself time to fly in and get there, particularly if the always unpredictable Colorado weather intervened.

So, he had left home five days before the proposed closing, and flown to Denver, where he'd rented an SUV and – since life was contrary that way – made a perfect trip to Silver Ridge, unhampered by bad weather of any kind.

In fact, the weather must have been unseasonably warm late, because the entire drive reminded him of the Autumns of childhood. The road was elevated, most of the way, cut into the side of a cliff on the right, with the left falling away in an expanse of slopes and valleys. Those were all covered in trees – probably Aspens. He'd never cared enough to find out – that had put on their glad autumn plumage and shone in red and gold, interrupted here and there by the brilliant jade of evergreens.

The air had a spicy-cinnammony tang too. It reminded him of when dad used to go hunting, to feel the freezer for winter. Noah had gone too, a few times, but only in his early teens, before he'd started studying seriously so he could be admitted to a university that would give him access to a decent law school.

If you'd asked him until right now, he'd have told you he didn't remember much of it, but he did: Dad waking him up before dawn; the nip in the air as they drank their black coffee; walking through the trees, carefully, quietly.

It wasn't so much killing the deer that he cared about. That had been a strictly utilitarian thing. Dad kept chickens, and a few goats, and even in the worst years he grew enough vegetables to give them enough food. But they'd have near to starved if they hadn't supplemented with venison every fall.

He found himself smiling – which was stupid, since at the time he'd found the whole thing infuriating – as he remembered dad's various money-making schemes that never came off. Like his attempt at growing an apple orchard. Last time that Noah had been home, ten years ago, those apple trees still were not tall enough to reach his waist, after more than a decade of growing. Between the thin air and the rare watering, those poor things had never had a chance.

Then there was the berry farm. Well, the berry bushes had come in right enough, but there had never been a single berry on them. Ten years ago, they'd been a thorny spiny mass extending about an acre South of the house, but no one had ever spotted a berry on it.

In a way, Noah supposed he should feel happy that his father had ever felt any affinity for cattle or pigs, or anything larger than a goat. The goats had done well enough, and even been milked fairly regularly.

Some of the chickens had gone feral and lived around the farm. When Noah was young egg hunts had been literal.

But he shuddered at the idea of feral herds of cattle. And the neighbors would not have appreciated feral pigs.

The thing was, he supposed, that dad tried. He just never reached the level of trying that his grandparents had managed. And even that, despite all the machinery, hadn't got them much past subsistence.

So, perhaps Dad had broken. But he suspected the truth was dad had broken when mom had left. Because that was always the way. Women left you holding the short end of the stick after taking all you were willing to give.

And it was while thinking that, that Noah had driven into town, with the setting sun gilding the general store and the few Victorians in what passed for a main street.

There was a B &B here somewhere. Or at least he thought so, because where would the woman be staying when she came for the signing? But he didn't need to do that, so he just stopped by the general store. If water was still the way it had been at the farm, and with it being unoccupied for six months, the pipes had likely gone rusty. They already were kind of rusty. So, he'd buy a couple of gallons of water. He wasn't sure he wanted to go anywhere to eat, but he'd still need to drink water.

The store looked exactly like he remembered, with everything from shoes to tobacco on neat shelves, and old Mr. Dumond behind the counter.

It brought back memories of browsing the shelves walking behind dad, seeing it all at kid-eye-level. For just a moment he wished he could go back and be six again, following dad around. Which was stupid. He didn't remember those days being particularly happy. But then, he still hadn't been hurt. Life was still beautiful and shiny, and everything was going to go well for him.

He was shocked when Mr. Dumond, who didn't even look any older, because he'd always looked ancient, looked up at him, smiled and said, "Hi Noah. Been up to the old homestead yet?"

"No. I figured I'd need some water."

Mr. Dumond gave him an odd look. "You'll like it. Your old man did some right nice improvements there."

Oh, dear, Noah thought as he got in the car.

He had no idea what he'd find when he got back home.

What he found, it turned out, was nothing much. The door opened with his key, and he just stopped himself shouting out "Dad, I'm home."

Light came on when he flicked the switch, which was good. He'd been paying the electrical bill, but it was still a relief. Dad had been in the hospital for three months, and then the house was vacant for six months, and the lightbulb might have burned out or something.

The kitchen looked suspiciously clean, and there was a note on the counter, "I left you milk, bread and eggs in the refrigerator. And there's canned soup on the shelf. If you need anything, call me."

He stared, blankly, at the signature, which definitely had an N and S but beyond that was completely indecipherable. If the note had been here since Dad had gone to the hospital, it would have dust on it. Actually, the kitchen was very clean, so someone had been here.

Noah frowned in confusion. Well, it was probably one of the neighbors. In Silver Ridge people were always doing things like that. Mowing each other's lawn, or plowing each other's driveway, or perhaps bringing a basket of food to someone stricken or a casserole to a home where someone died.

He felt mildly worried someone had the key but even that was not that surprising. After all, there were probably half a dozen people who had the key.

The bread was homemade. The milk smelled fine. There was butter in the freezer. He had bread and butter and milk for dinner.

It wasn't till he was falling asleep that the thought flitted through his mind that what was really weird was that they knew when he was expected back. Though the realtor had probably talked.

And he woke up curled on hard ground, under the trees. For just a moment, before fully awake, he was huge, and had a tail and wings, pulled close in. And then it was just him, curled up on the hard ground.

There was a smell of apples all around, and, looking up, he saw he was under apple trees. He sat up, startled.

His confusion came from two things. It had been several years since he'd had the dream-of-being-a-dragon that ended with him waking up some place he wasn't supposed to be. And.... Where the heck had these apple trees come from? They were proper size apple trees, and he suspected they'd had a bountiful crop, too.

The soil looked better than it had, too. But as he got up, he saw the house. Which was good, because if he had got to a neighbor's orchard it would have been a long time getting back.

As it was, walking naked and barefoot through the cold morning back to the house was not exactly unpleasant, just unnerving, as he wasn't sure that no one could see him, or that the person who'd left food for him wouldn't come to check on him.

But he made it all the way to the house undisturbed, took a shower, noting that the water was hot and didn't seem to run out even when he stood under it for untold minutes to ease the hurt in his muscles from cramped outdoor sleeping.

This had never happened in college. It had happened once in the city after Natalie left. He'd been lucky enough to wake up in a deserted parking lot, before anyone found him. But now? Why now?

He was wearing chinos and a t-shirt and making eggs and bacon when she showed up at the door. She looked like something out of a fairytale, with short hair cut in a pixie bob, jeans, a colorful t-shirt, and the pinkest cheeks and bluest eyes he'd ever seen. And she had a wicker basket on her arm.

He was so surprised to see her, that he didn't say anything for a moment. "I brought you some apple butter," she said. "I suppose technically the apples were yours, and I shouldn't have picked them, but they were going to go bad."

He blinked at her in confusion, as she set the basket with the jars of apple butter on the counter. They had little red-checkered cloth tops.

"Oh, I'm sorry," she said. "You have no idea who I am, of course. I'm Nell Sawyer, of course."

Nell Sawyer. The buyer. He blinked. She didn't look in the least like he'd imagined. Not an old Mother Earth type.

She laughed. "I know. I'm sorry. I should have told you the whole story."

Over breakfast – after he invited her – she did tell him the whole story. Apparently, she'd moved into Silver Ridge ten years ago after her own divorce. Right after his visit to town, in fact. She'd become friends with his father. She was an engineer and had spent time helping dad build irrigation systems.

"It was fun," she said. "I don't need a lot of money, you know? We sold a house, when we divorced, I bought a cottage outright. There was no big expense. And I learned to do stuff, like irrigation, and .... It was fun. And then we started selling stuff in the farmer's market. Preserves and things. ... And, well. My uncle gave me a little money to buy the farm, since—"

He got it. She'd put work in it, she wanted to buy it.

Suddenly and inexplicably the feeling came again that to sell would be to lose something, that he would never find again.

They talked, then walked all over the orchard. In the evening, as a light snow fell, she got steaks from her cottage, and cooked. She also brought more fresh bread.

Noah wanted to ask her to stay, but he couldn't. She had gone through a divorce. She was doing okay. And if he got her to stay, what would they do about the relationship? He had to go back home.

In the morning, he woke up in the orchard again, but not alone.

As he blinked awake, he realized that his eyes saw in colors he'd never seen before. And there was a hand on his muzzle. It was warm and soft against the hard scales.

He flapped his wings in confusion, but Nell spoke, "I saw you yesterday too. Does this happen often?"

He was caught between a desire to become human again, and the realization he'd be naked, and he didn't want her to see him naked. So instead of letting his body become human again, he made a sound like "woof," that sounded vaguely like yes.

Her hand patted his muzzle. "It doesn't look comfortable. I'll go back to the house. Join me when you're human."

He became human instantly, by an effort of will, and walked towards the house after her. She was gallant and stayed turned away as he walked past her.

When he came down from the shower, she was making eggs and bacon.

"It started when my mom left," he said. "I don't even remember mom very well. She left when I was in first grade. But that's when it started. Dad saw it, and— He never said anything about it. He'd just get water hot. It used to be much harder, you know? We had a dinky little water heater, and he only turned it on at times, and—" He poured all of it out, drinking cups of coffee which she refilled, silently. "And then.... It didn't happen again till Natalie left."

"Did it hurt very badly, when Natalie left?" she asked.

He shrugged. "We should never have married. I don't think she really wanted.... I think she was looking for something I couldn't be. Maybe no one could. She wanted to always love, have a fairytale honeymoon. Honeymoon, you know. And I— Perhaps it was my fault too. You see, dad always said women leave you sooner or later."

Nell laughed at that. "My husband left. He found someone more successful. Prettier. She was more like the wife for the life he wanted to live."

There was a moment of silence. He nodded.

She stayed around that day. She showed him the berry patch, which was much larger, and now producing. "Mostly we made jam from it. IT's impossible to sell them all fast enough, you know? But the jam sells." A moment of silence. "I have the chickens and the goats. I've been looking after them."

"You're welcome to the chickens and the goats."

They'd spent the day together, and the more time they spent together, the less he wanted to sell. Or leave.

They watched the Christmas Parade in Silver Ridge, and it was like nothing he'd ever seen. Well, not since he was little. The scripted parades of the city were nothing like this. There were elaborate parades, made by all the clubs in town. The one put together by the football team was mostly a truck draped in white sheets, with the entire team posing and holding up strings of lights. It was lame, and sweet, and it made him laugh. He'd never been a part of the parades or the floats. Not after high school. He'd been too busy trying to get into law school.

"Has it ever occurred to you," Nell asked that night, as they sat by the fire in his fireplace. "That you hoard your injuries? That you turn into the dragon so you can sleep on your injuries. I don't mean that as a bad thing. I think it's how you figured out how to survive. You were just a scared little boy. And you were never given the chance to heal. Your dad wasn't good at talking or .... Or expressing his love. But he did love you, you know?"

He'd gone to bed with that thought. Before going to bed, he'd gone into dad's room.

It looked exactly like he remembered, with dad's jeans and flannel shirts still hanging. He'd said he didn't want anything from here. He thought he was a different person.

He put his face against dad's shirts. They were laundered, but they still smelled faintly of dad, a smell that always reminded him of tobacco and molasses.

There was dad's desk in the corner. No computer. Dad had never got used to it. He opened the desk and stopped. There was a pile of written letters. Never folded. Never sent. He felt as though he should turn away, but the top one said, "Dear Noah."

He sat down and read. It took hours. Nell hadn't been joking that dad didn't know how to speak of his feelings, but he could write them.

In the letters, unlike the feeling he'd got from living with dad, he explained why Noah's mother had left: she was a singer and had felt a need to perform again. And she'd died two years after leaving. Dad had never told him that, but it explained why Mom had never written or called. Or maybe she had those two years.

He read until his eyes stung, until he reached the last letter. Dad talked about Nell, and what a difference she'd made to him, how she'd given him heart again.

"I like to dream that she meets you, and you two live in this house, and raise my grandchildren. I know it is foolish. You have your grand career. But it is a sweet dream. And even if you should be unhappy and one of you should have to leave, it is worth it. Love, however brief, is worth it. I never regretted marrying your mother. I know it would mean giving up your big, successful career. But a man can dream."

His big successful career. When was the last time he had enjoyed what he did? He could probably get a different job, do research remotely. It would be a big demotion, a loss in pay, but Silver Ridge was cheap.

Noah woke up in bed, almost shocked at it.

He reached for his phone on the bedside table and called Nell.

"Would you mind terribly if I didn't sell?"

She chuckled. "I don't know. Would I still be allowed to harvest the apples?"

"Sure. Sure," he said. "And.... Maybe teach me to make apple butter?"

She had taught him to make apple butter, and in summer they drove to the next largest touristic town to sell the produce and the preserves. Little by little they built up the orchard. And Noah discovered a taste for making specialty goat cheese which sold very well.

They got married in May, in the apple orchard.

He'd never turned into a dragon again. The hard mix of hurt and fear and paranoia about those who loved him leaving him was gone. There was nothing to hoard.

Noah remained human and with Nell raised human children, whose laugher echoed amid the apple trees in summer, and who made the worst possible Christmas floats in winter.

And as they sat by the fire, holding hands in winter, he could feel as if his father stood behind them, smiling.

About Author

Sarah was born (and raised)in Porto, Portugal, where at the age of eight she decided she wanted to live in Denver and be a writer.

No, she has no idea whatsoever why Denver.

Her understanding of the world, at the time, might be judged by the fact

that she thought Denver was by the sea.

At any rate, having married a mathematician from Connecticut, she made

her way to Denver in her late twenties.

She's raised two sons and a countless number of cats in the Rocky

Mountains, and overall feels no need to repine for the choice she made at

eight.

In a writing career spanning 20 years (so far) she's become a bestseller

and received two prestigious awards (Prometheus: for Darkship Thieves, and the

Dragon: for Uncharted, with Kevin J. Anderson.)

She's published over 30 novels and over 150 short stories, in genres

ranging from science fiction to mystery, to fantasy, to historical. At the

moment, she's not written children's books, men's adventure or romance. But she

makes no promises. As the mathematician has instructed her to warn "No

genre is safe from her."

If you want to keep up with news and new releases, join Sarah's Newsletter:

Schrodinger Path: https://sarah38d.substack.com/

Also By

Gentleman Takes a Chance

Family! Can't live with them and can't eat them. Tom Ormson, owner -- with his girlfriend -- of The George, a diner in downtown Goldport, Colorado is well on his way to becoming a responsible and respectable adult, despite his rough start and the fact that he turns into a dragon. But then the unpredictable Colorado weather, the ancient leader of a dragon triad and an even more ancient shifter-enforcer combine to destroy his home, put his diner at risk and attempt to kill him. All this, of course, has to happen while Tom's friend, Rafiel, is trying to solve a series of murders-by-shark at the city aquarium, and Tom's newly-reconciled father is attempting to move to Denver. Fasten your seat belts, a wild ride is about to begin.

Noah's Boy

Tom Ormson and Kyrie Smith are suffering the growing pains of young romance and young business people. Tom worries obsessively about the new fryer in the diner exploding. As though he didn't have enough on his mind, though, life decides it's time for a sabretooth with vengeance on her mind to come to town, and for the Great Sky Dragon to try to arrange a marriage for Tom.

Meanwhile, out at the old amusement park, the one with the really good wooden roller-coaster, a series of bizarre murders is taking place. And, as if that were not enough, Conan Lung, dragon shifter, ex-triad member and waiter extraordinaire starts his country singing career with an original song "If I Could Fly to You."

When Kyrie is kidnapped, it's all Tom can do to make sure he protects her while not eating anyone.

Sweet Alice

A Shifter Series Prequel Short Story.

Rafiel Trall is studying law enforcement, preparing to follow in the footsteps of his father and grandfather as a police officer in Goldport, when he shifts shape into a lion. Fearful of hurting his classmates, he goes back home. But at home, a crime awaits his solving. And once he solves it, he will never be the same.

Dipped, Stripped and Dead
A Dyce Dare Mystery

When she was six, Dyce Dare wanted to be a ballerina, but she couldn't stop tripping over her own feet. Then she wanted to be a lion tamer, but Fluffy, the cat, would not obey her. Which is why at the age of twenty nine she's dumpster diving, kind of. She's looking for furniture to keep her refinishing business going, because she would someday like to feed herself and her young son something better than pancakes.
Unfortunately, as has come to be her expectation, things go disastrously wrong. She finds a half melted corpse in a dumpster. This will force her to do what she never wanted to do: solve a crime.
Life is just about to get crazy... er... crazier. But at least at the end of the tunnel there might be a relationship with a very nice Police Officer.

A French Polished Murder
A Dyce Dare Mystery

When Dyce Dare decides to refinish a piano as a gift for her boyfriend, Cas Wolfe, the last thing she expects is to stumble on an old letter that provides a clue to an older murder. She thinks her greatest problems in life are that her friend gave her son a toy motorcycle, and that her son has become unaccountably attached to a neurotic black cat named Pythagoras. She is not prepared for forgotten murder to reach out and threaten her and very thing she loves, including her parents' mystery bookstore.

A Fatal Stain
A Dyce Dare Mystery

When Dyce Dare buys a table to refinish, the last thing she expects is to find a human blood stain under the amateurish finish. Whose blood is it? What happened to the person who bled on the table?

Helped and hindered by her fiance, Cas Wolfe, her friend Ben, her son E and an imaginary llama named Ccelly, Dyce must find the killer and the victim,before the killer finds her.

Deep Pink

Like all Private Detectives, Seamus Lebanon [Leb] Magis has often been told to go to Hell. He just never thought he'd actually have to go.

But when an old client asks him to investigate why Death Metal bands are dressing in pink – with butterfly mustache clips – and singing about puppies and kittens in a bad imitation of K-pop bands, Leb knows there's something foul in the realm of music.

When the something grows to include the woman he fell in love with in kindergarten and a missing six-year-old girl, Leb climbs into his battered Suburban and like a knight of old goes forth to do battles with the legions of
Hell.

This is when things become insane.... Or perhaps in the interest of truth we should say more insane.

Witchfinder

In Avalon, where the world runs on magic, the king of Britannia appoints a witchfinder to rescue unfortunates with magical power from lands where magic is a capital crime. Or he did. But after the royal princess was kidnapped from her cradle twenty years ago, all travel to other universes has been forbidden, and the position of witchfinder abolished. Seraphim Ainsling, Duke of Darkwater, son of the last witchfinder, breaks the edict. He can't simply let people die for lack of rescue. His stubborn compassion will bring him trouble and disgrace, turmoil and danger -- and maybe, just maybe, the greatest reward of all.